P9-DMT-914

Charlie Joe Jackson's Guide to Summer School

Tommy Greenwald

Charlie Joe Jackson's Guide to Summer Vacation

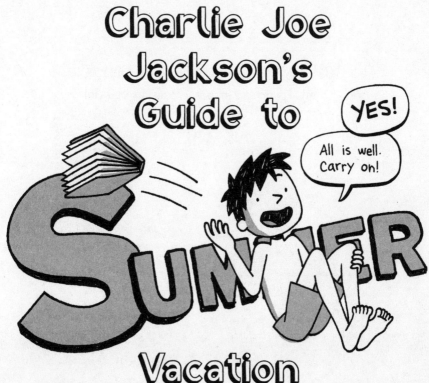

Illustrated by J.P. Coovert

Roaring Brook Press * New York

To Kenny and Ellen Greenwald

And to my favorite campers, Jessica and Jake

Text copyright © 2013 by Tommy Greenwald
Illustrations copyright © 2013 by J. P. Coovert
Published by Roaring Brook Press
Roaring Brook Press is a division of Holtzbrinck Publishing Holdings Limited Partnership
175 Fifth Avenue, New York, New York 10010
mackids.com

Library of Congress Cataloging-in-Publication Data

Greenwald, Tommy.
    Charlie Joe Jackson's guide to summer vacation / Tommy Greenwald ; illustrated by J. P. Coovert.—1st ed.
    p. cm.
    Summary: "Charlie Joe Jackson is back and he's at academic summer camp trying to convert all the other kids
to non-academics."—Provided by publisher.
    ISBN 978-1-59643-757-9 (hardcover) — ISBN 978-1-59643-880-4 (ebook)
[1. Camps—Fiction. 2. Interpersonal relations—Fiction. 3. Humorous stories.] I. Coovert, J. P., III II. Title.
    PZ7.G8523Chs 2013
    [Fic]—dc23

                                                                                        2012034249

Roaring Brook Press books may be purchased for business or promotional use. For more information on bulk
purchases please contact Macmillan Corporate and Premium Sales Department at (800) 221-7945 x54420.

First edition 2013
Book design by Andrew Arnold
Printed in the United States of America RR Donnelley & Sons Company, Harrisonburg, Virginia

10 9 8 7 6 5 4 3 2 1

Anyone who reads too much and uses his own brain too little falls into lazy habits of thinking.
—Albert Einstein

PROLOGUE

I guess the only thing I'll say before we get started is that I don't want you to worry. This isn't one of those summer vacation stories where there's some crazy killer on the loose who's hiding in the woods and picking off all the innocent kids one by one.

It's definitely not that bad.

Not quite, anyway.

✳ ✳ ✳

So here's the deal: At the end of the last school year, I went temporarily crazy, decided to make my parents happy, and agreed to spend three weeks at an academic summer camp called Camp Rituhbukkee.

Pronounced "Read-a-Bookie."

In other words, nerd camp.

The next thing I knew, I was in the car and on my way. I can barely remember the ride up—just that it was the longest four hours of my life. Saying good-bye to my mom and dad, my sister Megan, and my dogs, Moose and Coco, was also a total blur. I think I was in shock.

The first thing I really remember was looking around

the camp, and immediately wanting to turn around and go home.

It was like I'd crash-landed on the Planet of the Gifted Children.

There were very few signs of familiar human life. My unofficial best friend from home, Katie Friedman, had decided to come to the same camp, which was pretty awesome of her.  Nareem Ramdal, who was tied with Jake Katz for the nerdiest person I knew, had been going to this camp for years, so he was there, too. The rest of the population consisted of seventy-five of the smartest-looking kids I'd ever seen in my life. Plus a bunch of adults, who looked just as smart as the kids.

Books were everywhere. And cell phones and video games were nowhere. (Not allowed, of course.)

I looked around for the spaceship that would take me back to Planet Normal, but there wasn't one. Then I pinched myself, trying to make myself wake up from what I hoped was a terrible dream. That didn't work, either. Slowly I began to realize that there was no way out.

Like it or not, I was going to be stuck at Camp Rituhbukkee for the next three weeks.

DAILY CAMP SCHEDULE	
7 AM	*Breakfast*
8 AM	*First Workshop: Grammar and Style.*
9 AM	*Second Workshop: Reading Techniques.*
10 AM	*Third Workshop: The Write Stuff.*
11 AM	*Free Swim.*
12 noon	*Lunch.*
1 PM	*Quiet Hour 1. Reading and letter writing.*
2 PM	*First Rec.*
3 PM	*Second Rec.*
4 PM	*Water Sports.*
5 PM	*Quiet Hour 2: Reading and letter writing.*
6 PM	*Dinner.*
7 PM	*Evening activity.*
9 PM	*Quiet Hour 3: Reading and letter writing.*
10 PM	*Lights out.*

10:01 PM—weeping into my pillow.

Dear Mom and Dad,

One of the first things they told us at camp was that we're going to be writing a lot of letters. They say it will improve our "narrative skills," whatever they are.

    Anyway, our first letter home is supposed to tell you what we hope to accomplish at camp.

    I hope to learn how to stop making dumb decisions just to make your parents happy.

    Your loving son,

    Even though I'm not feeling all that loving right now,

Charlie Joe

Week One
CAMP JOCKSTRAP

I knew what the place was going to be like as soon as I saw the sign on the way in to camp.

CAMP RITUHBUKKEE: MOLDING YOUNG MINDS SINCE 1933

I'm sorry, but I don't want my mind to be molded. Mold is gross. It reminds me of that green stuff that grows on bread. I hate mold.

I'd prefer my mind deep fried, sprinkled with powdered sugar, and then covered in chocolate sauce.

On the surface, Camp Rituhbukkee looked like pretty much any other nice summer camp. It had a big lake for swimming, a basketball court, a tennis court, and baseball and soccer fields. The campers lived in cool log cabins in the woods, and the dining room was huge, with big wooden tables and chairs everywhere. There was a room for arts and crafts and stuff like that, and a theater where you put on shows.

It was actually a really nice place, if you were able to forget about what you were there to do.

Which was read and write.

Even though Katie and Nareem were at camp with me, I couldn't stop thinking about everybody else back home. Mostly I thought about the awesome and amazing Zoe Alvarez, my almost-girlfriend. She was the only girl who could ever compare to the awesome and amazing Hannah Spivero. I missed Zoe already, and I'd only been gone five hours. I also thought about the rest of the gang—Jake, Timmy, Pete, and yeah, Hannah. I pictured them at the beach, having a great time doing nothing; or at the movies, eating French fries and talking about what a loser I was. Which is exactly what I would have been doing if I were them.

Sadly, though, I wasn't them. I was me.

And so, instead of having a great time doing nothing, I found myself standing with all the other campers, in a giant circle around a flagpole. Because it was the first day, we had to do what was called the "Welcome Ring." Meaning, we all held hands and sang the camp song, which was called "Learning To Love, and Loving To Learn."

That's pretty much all you need to know about that song.

I stared at Katie and Nareem, who were singing at the top of their lungs. "Are you guys serious?"

Katie giggled. "Charlie Joe, you're at camp now," she said, while somehow managing to not miss a note. "Stop being such a Negative Norman and get with the program."

"But I'm not with the program," I explained. "I'm very much against the program."

"I still can't believe you decided to attend the camp, Charlie Joe," Nareem said. "You are not someone I normally associate with books and reading and learning."

"Ya think?" Katie added, which made them both giggle all over again.

I rolled my eyes and pretended to sing, until finally the song ended. Then an extremely tall man with extremely short shorts stepped into the center of the circle. All the kids clapped, until he put his hand up to stop them. They stopped immediately.

"Greetings, and welcome to Camp Rituh-bukkee!" the tall man announced. "Welcome back, to those many familiar faces I see. And to those newcomers, please allow me to introduce myself. My name is Dr. Malcolm Malstrom, but you can call me Dr. Mal. I'm not a medical doctor, though, so if you get sick, don't call me at all." He paused for laughter, and it came in a huge wave. Which was strange, since what he said wasn't actually funny.

"We're all excited for another wonderful season here at Rituhbukkee," Dr. Mal continued. "We've got many new surprises in store to make this our best summer ever."

I looked at Katie as if to say, *Seriously?*

She looked back at me as if to say, *Behave.*

Dr. Mal glanced down at his clipboard. "Before we go to our cabins to get settled in before dinner, I wanted to mention one last thing." He smiled like a dad who is about to give the most awesome present ever. "This year, we'll be introducing the Rituhbukkee Reward. This extraordinary honor will go to the one camper who best displays the camp's core values of integrity, community, and scholarship."

Everybody *ooh*-ed and *aahh*-ed.

"The winner of the Rituhbukkee Reward," Dr. Mal added, "will be awarded a full scholarship to camp next year, at absolutely no cost, and will be admitted to the counselor training program when he or she reaches the appropriate age."

The *ooh*s and *aahh*s turned into excited squeals of delight. Even Katie and Nareem were nodding happily.

"Sounds more like a punishment than a reward," I whispered, a little too loudly. The girl on my left looked at me like I'd just eaten a plate of fried slugs.

Katie tried to shush me, but it was too late—it turned out that Dr. Mal had really good hearing.

He walked over to me. "Hello, young man."

I looked up at him. He was really tall. His face was a long ways up. "Hello, sir."

"Call me Dr. Mal," he said, smiling. "What's your name?"

"Charlie Joe Jackson."

"Ah yes," said Dr. Mal, nodding. "Mr. Jackson. You come to us with a bit of a reputation."

"Thanks," I said, even though I was pretty sure it wasn't a compliment.

"I'm glad you're here, even if you consider it a punishment," said Dr. Mal, putting his big hand on my shoulder. "Can you tell us what it is you hope to learn here at Camp Rituhbukkee?"

I said the first thing that popped into my head, which was exactly what I told Timmy and Pete, my friends back home, when they asked me the same thing.

"I hope to learn how to read while napping."

Everyone gasped, then went silent. Nobody moved. I think even the birds stopped chirping.

Oops.

Katie gave me the classic eye-roll.

But Dr. Mal never stopped smiling. "So you're not a fan of reading."

"Nope," I said proudly. "In fact, I've pretty much never read a book all the way through, except under emergency circumstances beyond my control."

I expected the kids to laugh, like they usually did when I made a joke. Instead, they all just stared at me. Some were even whispering to each other, pointing at me, like *who is this guy?*

I did notice one kid who looked like he was about to

laugh—but he was wearing a Harvard T-shirt, so I immediately ruled him out as a fellow book-hater.

Dr. Mal nodded again. "In that case, do you mind if I ask you why you've joined us here at camp?"

"Good question, Dr. Mal. I guess I did it to make my parents happy. It was a moment of weakness, to be honest with you."

That line would have gotten a laugh back home too, for sure. But not here. It was like I'd entered some kind of permanent Opposite Day, where the dorks were the cool kids, and the cool kids—or at least the funny kids—were the outsiders.

Dr. Mal looked down at his clipboard again, then nodded at a big guy who was standing across the circle. "It seems you'll be in with Dwayne, who's one of our best counselors." Dwayne nodded back without smiling. He was by far the least nerdy-looking guy at the whole place. He looked more like a marine than a counselor.

Dr. Mal headed back to the center of the ring. "You may find, Charlie Joe, that you're more like your fellow campers than you realize," he said. Then he looked me right in the eyes and added, "We'll make you one of us yet."

Make you one of us?

Oh, please. I would never become one of them.

But . . . I started thinking . . . maybe I could make *them* one of *me*!

I realized it would at least be a way to make the next three weeks bearable. I could help these kids change their ways. I could turn them into normal, non-reading people. I would save them from a life of dorkdom.

The next thing on the fun-filled agenda was to unpack. Nareem and I started walking down the path to our cabin.

"I think you may have gotten off on the wrong foot with Dr. Mal," Nareem said. "He's actually a really good person. I think you'll like him once you get to know him a little better."

Before I could compliment Nareem on his optimism, two kids came running up. One was the tallest kid I've ever seen in my life, and the other was the Harvard T-shirt kid who'd almost laughed at my joke during the Welcome Ring.

Judging by the way they ran, I was pretty sure neither of them were the captains of their football teams back home, if you know what I mean.

"Nareem!" they both shouted.

Nareem broke into a huge grin. "Dudes!"

They did that weird half-handshake-half-hug thing that friends do when they haven't seen each other for a while.

"Charlie Joe, I want you to meet George Feedleman and Jack Strong, two of my best buddies here at camp."

George was the giant one. I shook his hand first.

"Hey," I said.

"Nice to meet you," George said. "Welcome to camp, the most awesome place on earth."

I did a private eye-roll but tried to play nice. "Yeah, cool."

"George is the smartest human being on the planet," Nareem announced.

"That's great," I said.

The Harvard T-shirt kid stuck out his hand. "Jack Strong."

I looked at his scrawny body. "Is that really your last name?"

Jack blushed. "I know, it doesn't really fit."

"I wasn't thinking that," I lied.

Jack smiled. "You were pretty funny at the Welcome Ring."

"Thanks," I said. "But not funny enough to make anybody actually laugh, I guess."

Jack shrugged. "And get in trouble on the first day? Are you serious?"

"Not usually."

That time he actually did laugh.

I pointed at his Harvard shirt. "What's that about?"

"Oh, nothing," Jack said. "I might apply there someday. It's super hard to get in, though."

"Isn't it a little early to be worrying about stuff like that?" I asked.

"Jack thinks about colleges a lot," George interrupted. "Or should I say, his dad does. He's super-intense about that kind of stuff."

Jack looked embarrassed for the second time in eight seconds, so I decided to change the subject. "Guys," I said, "Nareem here says that Dr. Mal is a great guy. Can that actually be possible?"

"It can," said George.

"It totally can," said Jack.

Okay, so that's how it was going to be.

"Dr. Mal asked a good question," Jack added. "Why *are* you here? You said it was to make your parents happy, but is that really the only reason?"

"I'm also hoping to meet some awesome girls," I said. "Can you guys help with that?"

Nareem, George, and Jack looked at each other.

"No," they all said, at the same exact time.

Our cabin, which held eight campers, was called the Roald Dahl cabin. (All the cabins were named after famous authors, btw. I was just glad I wasn't in the Mark Twain cabin. He and I haven't gotten along ever since my sixth birthday was ruined, when my dad gave me the entire Mark Twain collection as my only present. I still shiver just thinking about it.)

When we walked in, the other four kids were busy unpacking. I introduced myself around. They all seemed like okay kids, but I could tell they were all a little weirded out by my argument with Dr. Mal. They definitely weren't used to having a non-reader among them. Plus, they each had at least one really weird habit:

- Eric Cunkler spoke three languages, but barely talked at all.
- Jeremy Kim sneezed about twenty times a minute and kept a year's supply of tissues under his bed.
- Kenny Sarcofsky had decided he'd live foverer if he ate a lot of garlic, so he smelled a little "different."
- Sam Thurber never changed his underwear (according to Nareem) but already had a short story published in *The New Yorker* magazine.

And then there was Nareem, George, and Jack, whom you've already met, and our counselor, Dwayne, who actually seemed like a pretty cool guy, in an "if you mess up I will kill you" kind of way.

Anyway, that's my cabin and the kids who were in it. Sounds like quite a gang, right? Do you want to guess who was the outsider in the bunch?

That's right.

Me.

Dear Zoe,

I've been at camp for two days already! I can't believe how fast the time is flying by!
   Not.
   How are you? I'm so glad I got to know you this year. I think it's good we decided not to go out while I'm at camp, though, don't you? But that doesn't mean we can't go to the movies or something when I get back. Hopefully that's okay with you.
   Katie and Nareem say hi. They love it here, which I'll try not to hold against them. They hang around together a lot, by the way. As for me, I haven't exactly made a ton of friends so far. I think some of the kids might even consider me a bad influence. I don't know where they get that idea from.
   Write back soon. Hopefully we can hang around together when I get home. Let me know about the movies thing.

Your friend,
Charlie Joe

So one of the first things I realized was that if I was going to make the other kids less nerdy, I had to start slowly. It's not like I could convince the entire camp to hate reading and writing in one day. I needed to take it one camper at a time. I started with the biggest, brainiest, and tallest genius of them all.

George Feedleman.

Rumor had it that George's IQ was so high it broke the machine. George was one of those kids who was so smart, he understood things on some super secret level. Kind of like the way dogs hear sounds.

It was the second day of camp, and we were in The Write Stuff workshop. I'd plopped down in the back row, which was traditionally my favorite row.

No one joined me.

"Lots of room here, people," I said. "The back row is where all the action is."

No one cared.

Eventually, I got Katie and Nareem to sit next to me. "Don't worry," Katie said, patting my knee. "They'll eventually get used to your strange ways."

George sat two rows in front of us. About ten minutes

into class, I decided to make my move. I tossed a wadded-up piece of paper at him.

"Pssst!"

No response.

"Pssst!" I said again, a little louder. The other kids started staring at me. Finally George turned around.

"What?" he said, with irritation in his genius eyes. Even though we'd had a few conversations, he was still suspicious of my un-studious nature, like everybody else.

I pointed at George's paper. "What are you working on?"

He shrugged. "Nothing. Just an analysis of class structure in the works of Emily Brontë."

"Emily who?"

"No one," George said, turning back to his work.

"Cool," I said. Then, after a small pause, I added, "I'm writing a letter to this girl back home."

"You are relentless," Katie whispered at me, her eyes never leaving her paper.

"Is 'relentless' good?" I asked her.

"No."

I turned my attention back to George. "Her name's Zoe."

He looked up. I could tell he was interested, even though he didn't want to be. "Is she your girlfriend?"

"Nah. I mean, we kind of like each other, but we're not going out or anything."

George nodded. "Good for you."

He glanced nervously at the workshop leader (or what in normal society would be called a teacher), whose name was Ms. Domerca. I'm pretty sure George had never talked in class in his entire life, unless it was to correct teachers when they were wrong.

Ms. Domerca seemed really nice and funny. She also dressed in the craziest clothes I've ever seen in my life. She was busy helping another kid out with his paper, so the coast was clear.

"What about you?" I asked George. "Do you have a girl-friend?"

George looked at me as if I'd just asked him if he had a dead body buried in his backyard.

Before he could answer, a really cute girl with red hair named Cathy Ruddy shot daggers at me with her eyes. "Leave him alone, he's working," she said. "You should try it sometime."

I smiled at her, but she didn't smile back.

"Do you?" I asked George again.

He threw his pencil down. "No I don't have a girlfriend! Um, I mean, not yet. I'm totally planning on getting one next year, though."

"What are you waiting for? There are a lot of really nice girls right here at camp." I pointed at Cathy. "Did you see how Cathy just stuck up for you? I bet she would go out with you."

"What makes you think that?" said a voice that was definitely not George's. Or Cathy's.

I looked up. Ms. Domerca was standing over me in her green and orange shirt.

"Hi," I said.

Ms. Domerca laughed. "Two days in, and I already know who my troublemaker is. Usually it takes a week, at least." Then she pointed at George and me. "Back to work, both of you," she said, as she walked away.

"Thanks a lot," whispered George.

"No problem," I said. George shook his head and turned back to his paper.

I wasn't done, though.

"Pssst!" I said again, this time to Cathy Ruddy.

"What is wrong with you?" she hissed.

"Would you consider going out with the smartest kid in America?" I asked her.

"I'm assuming you don't mean you."

"Right."

Cathy took a long look at George.

"Maybe," she said. "But only if you leave us both alone."

George stared down at his paper, his face turning bright red. Then he looked at Cathy, and for just a second, it seemed like he couldn't care less about class structure in the works of Emily Brontë.

Like I said, people, one camper at a time.

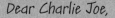

Dear Charlie Joe,

Thanks for writing so fast! I miss you. The summer's just not the same without you. But we're managing to have a really fun time anyway! Don't get mad.

I think it's cool that you have to write letters instead of just texting people all the time. My mom says it reminds her of when she was a kid.

Things here are going pretty good, I'm painting a lot and just hanging around with friends and stuff. Actually it gets a little boring sometimes, but you would probably think it's perfect. I like to stay busy, though. Tomorrow we are going to visit my dad. My parents talk to each other now more than they did when they were married, which is pretty weird. We'll see what happens.

I'll write again soon, I promise.

XO
Zoe

Here's the one thing I discovered that's kind of good about this camp: It took about five minutes to realize I was the best athlete in the whole place.

Yup. It turns out that when you go to a camp filled with kids who would rather write a paper than throw a baseball, you're considered a real superstar if you can run fifty feet without falling down. Who knew? It was kind of ridiculous, but I liked it.

On the fourth day of camp, we were playing basketball during First Rec when I saw my counselor Dwayne heading over to me. Dwayne was kind of like a nice Mr. Radonski (my crazy gym teacher back home). Dwayne was very large, very loud, and very intense. He was also the basketball coach, which basically meant it was his responsibility to make sure the kids didn't hurt themselves with the balls.

"Hey, Charlie Joe," he said.

I tossed in a five-footer. "What's up?"

"Have you heard about the big game with Camp Wockajocka?"

You bet I had. Camp Wockajocka was a favorite topic of conversation at meals. Kids called it "Camp Jockstrap."

It was about ten miles up the road, and they came to our camp every summer for a basketball game. They always killed us, of course. One was a real camp, and one was a summer school in disguise.

"Sure," I said. "Why?"

Dwayne watched Nareem shoot an air ball, then turned back to me. "I want you to captain this year's team," he said. "The game is this Saturday, and I don't want to be embarrassed."

"Seriously? I'm the new guy. What about somebody who's been coming to camp longer?"

Dwayne laughed a sad little laugh. "Have you seen them play?"

He had a good point.

"So how about it?" asked Dwayne. "You in?"

Just then, Jared Bumpers came running over. He was one of the kids I was talking about, a little older than me, who'd been coming to camp forever, and I could already tell he was that obnoxious type who thought he was awesome. "What are you guys talking about?"

"I'm asking Charlie Joe if he wants to be captain of the team," Dwayne told him.

Jared looked shocked.

"Charlie Joe is an excellent player," Dwayne continued. "But I'm counting on you too, Jared." Dwayne looked back at me. "So what do you say?"

I felt a little like I was being asked to steer the *Titanic* around the iceberg, but what the heck. It was something to do, and maybe I could make a friend or two along the way.

"Sure, why not," I said.

"This isn't fair," Jared said. "I'm older, I should be captain."

"You're captain of the debate club," Dwayne pointed out.

"Debate club has a captain?" I asked, which seemed to make Jared even madder.

He snorted. "Whatever," he said, and stomped away just as Jack Strong walked up.

"What's his problem?" I asked.

"Ignore him," Jack said. "He's always been totally annoying. People think it's because his older brother was like

28

this genius camp legend, and Jared isn't, and he's kind of bitter about it."

"That's enough about Jared," Dwayne said. Then he smacked me on the back. "Ready, Captain?"

"Not really," I said. "What do I have to do?"

"Figure out a way to beat the bad guys," said Dwayne, his face starting to twitch. His face always twitched when he got excited, which was about eighty percent of the time.

"I'll put my best men on it," I said.

"That's what I'm worried about," Dwayne said.

Dear Zoe,

It was so awesome to hear from you!
  I hope you had a great time at your dad's house. I want to hear all about it, so when you have a chance, please write me back as soon as you can.
  I was also glad to hear you are painting. You are an amazing painter, and I bet you'll become famous one day.
  Things at camp are not as bad as I thought they would be, but that doesn't necessarily mean that they are good, either. Please write back soon. Oh wait, I said that already.

I miss you, too.

Charlie Joe

That night before dinner, Jack, George, and I sat on the steps outside the cabin, munching on the amazing chocolate chip cookies that Jack's grandmother sent.

"How can you be so skinny if your grandma makes cookies like this?" I asked Jack.

"I have no idea," he said.

I pointed at his shirt, which said Stanford on it. "What's up with the college T-shirts?"

Jack glanced down at his shirt and suddenly looked self-conscious. "My dad went here."

"Did he go to Harvard, too?"

"Actually, yeah," Jack said. "Business school."

"Ssshhh, you two," George said.

It was Quiet Hour, and technically we were all supposed to be in our bunks reading, but I'd convinced Dwayne to let me sit outside if I promised to keep quiet. Since George and Jack were the only kids in my cabin besides Nareem who treated me like a person, instead of some sort of mysterious, anti-learning alien life form, they sat outside with me. George had decided I was okay after I introduced him to Cathy Ruddy, a real live girl; and

Jack was just a nice kid, who didn't hold my evil habits against me.

I decided to repay their friendliness by doing everything I could to distract them from their reading.

"Where's Nareem?" I asked.

George pointed up the hill. "He's with Katie in the library."

"That doesn't seem fair," I said, feeling a little annoyed for some reason. "Everyone's supposed to be in their cabins during Quiet Hour."

Jack looked at me. "Why, you'd rather be in the library?"

George laughed. "Dr. Mal said it was okay, since they're working on a project together."

I shrugged. "Whatever."

"Although now that you mention it," Jack said, "Nareem and Katie do seem to hang out together a lot." He looked at George. "Kind of like you and Cathy Ruddy." George blushed intensely. He looked as if he didn't know whether to be embarrassed or excited, so he decided to be both.

I chomped on a cookie, thinking about what Jack had said. I'd also noticed that Katie and Nareem were together a lot since camp began, but I thought I might just be imagining it because they were the only kids I knew.

I decided it wasn't worth thinking about and changed the subject. "You two guys are the smartest people I know,"

I said. "You gotta help me come up with a way to beat Camp Jockstrap."

Neither one said anything.

"Why are we even talking about this?" Jack asked. "The idea is to just get past it as quickly as possible, and remember that eventually we'll get into better schools than they will."

"Dude, you need to relax about this whole college thing," I told him.

"Relaxing isn't part of his dad's master plan," George said.

"My dad doesn't have anything to do with it," Jack said defensively. "It's just good to think ahead, that's all."

"Well, I don't care about thinking ahead," I said, "and neither does Wockajocka."

George looked up from his book. "What about deflating the ball by five percentage points? According to a study I once read called 'Proper Inflation of a Basketball,' by Josephine Corcoran and Ralph Rackstraw, 'A basketball is correctly inflated when it rebounds to approximately 60 percent of the height from which it is dropped.' So, if we deflate the ball, it will not rebound into their hands properly, and their game will be thrown off accordingly."

I stared at him. "Why did you read a study about the inflation of a basketball, and how do you remember exactly what it was called and who wrote it?"

George shrugged. "I just did, and I just do," he said, as if it were the most obvious thing in the world.

"Anyway, we can't do that," I pointed out. "It might throw their game off, but it will throw our game off, too."

"Can you throw off a game that isn't on in the first place?" Jack wondered.

George shook his head. "Not last I checked."

"You guys aren't helping," I complained. "I know you're brainiacs and everything, but life is about a lot more than just grades and books and studying." I got up and started pacing like a coach in one of those sports movies where the underdog beats the bad guys to win the championship. "It's about figuring out a way to win. It's about beating the odds. It's about David kicking Goliath's—"

The cabin door swung open. I looked up to see Jeremy Kim standing in the doorway, with a book in one hand and a tissue in the other. Sam Thurber, Kenny Sarcofsky, and Eric Cunkler were right behind him.

"Hey, can you please keep it down?" Jeremy asked politely. "It's hard to concentrate."

I wasn't sure if he was kidding or not. "Seriously?"

"Seriously," Eric said. "I know it's not easy for you to understand, but some of us actually enjoy reading quietly."

"We'd just appreciate it if you lowered your voices a bit," Kenny said, garlic breath accompanying every word.

"Yeah, no offense or anything, but you're being a little

loud," Sam added. They all nodded, then Jeremy topped things off with a sneeze.

It was almost like they were speaking a foreign language.

"Guys," I said, "I don't want you to take this the wrong way, but you are not normal. In fact, you're kind of the opposite of normal."

"QUIET!" Dwayne barked suddenly from inside the cabin.

"We're trying to figure out how to beat Camp Jockstrap like you asked," I yelled in to him.

"Well, figure it out softer," Dwayne grumbled. "And P.S., I didn't expect you to actually come up with something that would work."

My four opposite-of-normal cabinmates went back inside.

"We should probably hit the books, too," Jack said.

"Oh no, you don't," I protested. "You guys are my only friends in this whole place."

"What about Katie and Nareem?" Jack asked.

"They're too busy writing papers together," I said.

The sound of someone singing made us turn around. It was Nareem, heading down the path to our cabin. The singing was a complete violation of Quiet Hour rules.

"Ssshhh!" I said, annoyed at his happiness for some reason. "You'll get us all in trouble!"

George and Jack looked at me funny, since I was already known more as a trouble-creator than a trouble-avoider.

Nareem smiled. "Sorry, everyone."

"Someone's in a good mood," Jack said, grinning at Nareem.

"Yeah, I wonder why," George added.

"I am indeed," Nareem said. "Katie and I made excellent progress on our work."

"I'll bet you did," George said, elbowing Nareem in the ribs. Everyone laughed, except me.

"That's fantastic, Nareem, good for you," I said. "But meanwhile, I've got to figure out a way to win an unwinnable basketball game."

Nareem put his backpack down, took out a cookie, and started chomping thoughtfully. "Oh yes, that is a tricky one," he said. "You know what makes me particularly irate? That we have to lose to someone like Teddy Spivero. The rest of the kids at Camp Jockstrap aren't so bad, but he's the worst."

I dropped my cookie.

There were two things wrong with what Nareem had just said.

One, I didn't know what "irate" meant.

And two? *TEDDY SPIVERO.*

I stared at Nareem and started pacing around the porch. "What did you just say about Teddy Spivero?"

He looked surprised. "You mean you didn't know? We

36

play him every year. Teddy goes to Camp Wockajocka. Hannah's brother."

"Duh," I snapped. "I know who he is." Teddy Spivero happened to be my archenemy, practically since birth. He was definitely the most annoying person ever created. Which was particularly shocking, since his twin sister Hannah was tied with Zoe Alvarez for the most perfect creature ever created. Teddy had made it his mission in life to embarrass me in front of his sister. And many times, I'm sorry to say, it was mission accomplished.

I still couldn't quite believe what Nareem was saying. "Teddy goes to Camp Jockstrap?"

"Yes," Nareem said. "He's one of their best players."

You gotta be kidding me. Teddy Spivero, Camp Jockstrap basketball star. This was the worst news I'd had all summer, which was really saying something. It was bad enough being on a team of nerds who were about to get killed by a bunch of jocks. Now it turned out my own personal worst nightmare was their head jock.

But Jack was smiling. "This might not be such a bad thing," he said.

I looked at him like he had two heads. "What are you talking about?"

"Think about it," Jack added, which was the most popular expression at camp, since the kids at Camp Rituhbukkee loved to think about everything. "You've known this guy like your whole life. You must know a lot about him. So, there must be something, some weakness he has, which we can use to our advantage." He got up to put the cookies away, but I grabbed one first. "Think about it," he repeated, closing the box.

I did what he said—I thought about it. And then I thought about it some more. And the more I thought, the more I realized he was right. I did know a lot about Teddy Spivero, from studying his sister so carefully all these years. I knew what he liked. I knew what he disliked.

And best of all, I knew what his two major obsessions were.

A plan started forming in my head.

"George," I said, "do you think your girlfriend Cathy would do me a favor?"

"She's not my girlfriend, but yes, if I ask her to," George answered immediately, not blushing this time. Jeez. A little attention from a cute red-haired girl, and suddenly he was Mr. Confidence.

"Cool." I went to the door. "Dwayne, come out here!" I'd be waking him up, but I didn't care. Quiet Hour would have to wait.

The rest of the guys came running out of the cabin,

looking at me like I was insane. Kind of like the way I looked at them when they told me to quiet down so they could read.

Then Dwayne stumbled out, with his eyes half closed.

"What is it, Jackson?" he said, opening Jack's cookie box and grabbing a handful. "This better be good."

"Oh, it's good all right," I said. I was feeling pretty proud of myself. In fact, if I could have patted myself on the back, I would have.

"I think I might have a way we can win this game."

I told everyone my plan, with Nareem, George, and Jack helping me perfect it along the way. The other kids thought it was ridiculous, but Dwayne just sat there, looking at me intensely.

When I finished, Dwayne got up and walked around the porch for a minute, not saying anything. I could tell that he was trying to decide between trusting some crazy kid he barely knew and being willing to try anything to win.

When a weird half-smile crossed his face, I knew he'd made his decision.

"If this works," Dwayne told me, "you just might be the biggest genius here."

Then his booming laugh brought Quiet Hour to a close once and for all.

Dear Jake,

How's your summer going? Don't answer that.
   Camp Rituhbukkee is pretty much what I
thought it was going to be: a lot of reading, a
lot of writing, and a lot of people that remind
me of you.
   Katie and Nareem are good. I'm pretty sure
they like each other. Some other kids think so,
too. But so far they haven't said anything
about it. We'll see what happens.
   By the way, I'm playing your girlfriend's
brother's camp in basketball tomorrow.
How is Hannah, anyway? Please check one:
a) miserable
b) horrible
c) I don't know, because we broke up.

Your bud,

Charlie Joe

"Announcements! Quiet please, for announcements!"

Dr. Mal did announcements after every meal. They were usually about a wonderful short story he'd just read, or some new novel that he thought all the campers would love. (It's a good thing announcements didn't come before meals, because I might have lost my appetite.) But tonight's announcement was different.

"As we all know," he began, "tonight is our first Friday Night Campfire, and tomorrow is our annual visit with the fine young men of Camp Wockajocka."

Massive booing.

"You mean Camp Jockstrap!" yelled a voice in the back.

Massive cheering.

Dr. Mal made the calm-down motion with his hand. "I know, I know, they have given us a great deal of trouble on the basketball court in recent years, but try to remember, it's not about the final score, it's about learning how to play fair, hard, and with dignity. These are lessons that every student must learn, to take with them both on the field of play and in their chosen field of study."

This guy was unbelievable. Did everything have to be about studying?

"In any event, Coach Dwayne has told me that he expects big things this year," continued Dr. Mal. "I'd like to invite him up to the microphone to offer a few words of encouragement. Please welcome Coach Dwayne."

Dwayne wasn't quite as tall as Dr. Mal, so he had to lower the mike a little. "Since I know everyone here is into books, let me just say that tomorrow will begin a new 'chapter' in our rivalry with Camp Wockajocka," he said. We all started cheering like crazy, but he hushed us. "I don't want to give away our strategy, but all I can say is, COME HUNGRY!"

After he yelled those last two words, the place went nuts. Dwayne winked at me and started heading back to our table, but then remembered something and went back to the microphone.

"Oh, one last thing. I'd like to see Cathy Ruddy after dinner for just a minute, please. Thanks."

The whole dining hall turned to look at Cathy, whose face turned the color of the beets that they always served that I never ate.

Nareem leaned over to me. "You really think this is going to work?"

"Yeah, do you?" asked George.

"You guys might be the smartest kids in the country," I said, "but when it comes to fool-proof plans, I'm pretty much Albert Einstein."

Dear Charlie Joe,

You forgot one multiple choice for Hannah:
d) she's doing really well and we're still going
out. Sorry about that. But we both wish you
were around to hang out with.

 I hope camp is great and you aren't
regretting the decision to go. I saw your mom
walking Moose and Coco the other day and
she told me how proud she was of you. So just
hang in there for a couple more weeks, and
you can come home and totally do whatever
you want and not get in trouble.

 Awesome about Katie and Nareem. It
seemed kind of like they liked each other during
school so I'm not surprised that it's turning out
to be true. You must be so psyched for them,
huh?

 See you soon.

Jake

Friday Night Campfires were a big deal at Camp Rituhbukkee.

"Even if you hate the rest of camp," Nareem told me, "you'll love the campfires."

"*Hate* is a strong word," I replied. "I prefer 'would rather be anywhere else.'"

After dinner, everyone walked from the dining hall down a long dirt road to a clearing by the lake, where there was a huge fire climbing to the sky.

I had to admit, it was pretty cool.

All the campers sat in a giant circle. George was working his semi-magic with Cathy; Jack was with the other guys from my cabin, who were still a little suspicious of my non-reading ways; so I sat with Katie and Nareem, as usual. They were sitting very close to each other. Closer-than-just-friends close, if you ask me. Also sitting with us was Lauren Rubin, a quiet girl who was becoming one of Katie's good friends. Lauren was reading a book. I know—shocking, right?

Katie pinched my arm. "So what are you up to, Captain Charlie Joe?"

"Ow," I answered. "What do you mean?"

"I mean, I saw Dwayne wink at you during announce-ments. I figure you guys have something up your sleeve for the basketball game, and I want to know what it is."

"Aren't you a smarty-pants?"

"I am, in fact."

"Well, I'd tell you, but then I'd have to kill you."

Lauren smiled slightly behind her book.

"Charlie was very interested to learn that Teddy Spivero went to Camp Jockstrap," Nareem mentioned.

"Aha," said Katie, thinking that one over. She turned to Lauren. "Teddy is the obnoxious twin brother of the famous Hannah Spivero. Charlie Joe has had a crush on Hannah ever since he was old enough to say the words, 'I have a crush on Hannah.'"

"*Used* to," I explained. "I'm so over her now, though, it's not even funny."

"He met a great girl named Zoe this year," Katie explained, "and all of a sudden Hannah is yesterday's news."

"I see," Lauren said, still not looking up from her book.

I stared at the fire. Katie mentioning Zoe made me miss her a little, so I decided to change the subject.

"So what's up with you two?" I asked Nareem and Katie. "I watched you guys in school all year long, and now at camp. Something's going on."

"We're engaged," Katie said, which made Nareem spit juice out of his mouth.

"I hope you two will be very happy," Lauren said. They all giggled.

"Ha ha," I said, sarcastically. For some reason I didn't think the topic of Katie and Nareem was all that hilarious. I just wanted them to tell the world they liked each other, so we didn't have to spend the rest of our lives guessing.

Lauren looked up at me for the first time. "You're the kid who hates to read, right?"

Before I could say anything, Katie said, "Supposedly."

I looked at her. "What's that supposed to mean?"

"It means, I have a theory about why you came to camp," Katie said. "I know you say you did it for your parents, which is partly true. But it's not the only reason."

This got Lauren to shut her book.

"Here we go," I said, sighing. Even though I had no idea what Katie was getting at, her theories usually involved things I didn't want to hear.

Katie, meanwhile, was just getting warmed up. "You go around telling people how much you hate to read," she said, "and how you want to make us all less nerdy and more like you, but I'm not sure I believe you."

I scratched my head, not sure if I'd heard her correctly. I'd been accused of a lot of things in my life, but being a secret reader was never one of them. "Sorry, but that makes no sense," I said. "I don't like homework, I don't like school—well, I like the fun parts of school, like recess, but not the working part—and I definitely don't like reading."

"I'm not saying you like it," Katie said. "I'm saying there's a part of you that's fascinated by smart people, people who actually like to learn. Most of your friends back home are really smart, did you ever think about that? Jake, Nareem, Hannah, and, if I do say so myself, me."

"Pete Milano's not smart," I said, referring to my friend back home who specialized in C's and D's. But Katie was too busy getting ready for her big finish to hear me.

"I think that deep down," she announced, "some part of you actually wants to be a nerd."

I had no idea what to say. I was totally shocked. Who wouldn't be? It was the craziest thing I'd ever heard in my life. Yes, I liked having smart friends, but that was because they could help me with my homework and stuff. And besides, so what?

Suddenly I felt mad. "If you don't want to hang around with me at camp, Katie, then you should just say so."

"Don't overreact," she said.

"How am I overreacting?" My voice was getting a little louder. I pointed at Nareem. "You've been hanging around with Nareem way more than me. Why is that? Is it because he belongs here and I don't? Either that, or you like each other. So maybe you should figure out whether or not you and him are actually going to become boyfriend and girlfriend, instead of coming up with random theories that you know will annoy me."

Katie looked a little hurt.

"That wasn't nice, Charlie Joe," Nareem said quietly.

"Sorry," I said, trying to sound like I meant it.

All of a sudden somebody started banging on a cow-bell.

"Boys and girls, let's sing!" yelled Ms. Domerca, who was standing in front of the bonfire, wearing a purple dress with apples and oranges on it.

I looked at Nareem, who shrugged. "Ms. Domerca loves sing-alongs."

She launched into a slightly out-of-tune version of "Blowin' in the Wind." After an awkward minute, Katie put her hand on my shoulder. "You know, even if you are a secret nerd, I still love you," she said.

"Stop calling me that," I said back to her. "I mean it."

Katie looked at me, shook her head, then walked away. After a second, Nareem followed her.

I watched them go, not sure what to do. Katie and I had barely ever argued before, and it felt weird, in a bad way. I wanted to take it back, but it was too late now.

Lauren was still sitting on a log, reading. She was like a girl version of Jake Katz—nice, smart, shy, and always with a book in her hand. But she reminded me of Jake Katz before he started going out with Hannah, and became a lot more confident. Lauren didn't have all that much confidence, as far as I could tell.

I looked down at her. "What are you reading?"

Lauren held up the cover. "*The Miracle Worker.*" Then she smiled at me. "It's a play. Does that make it any better?"

"What's that supposed to mean?"

"It means I know how much you hate books," Lauren said, then she smiled. "Or do you?"

"Can we stop talking about that, please?" I snapped.

Lauren's face turned bright red. "Sorry. I was just making a dumb joke." She looked away, embarrassed.

I wanted to say I was sorry, too, that it wasn't her I was mad at. It was Katie and her annoying theories, and Zoe for being far away, and all my friends back home for having fun without me, and this whole place, where I felt totally out of place for the first time in my life. I wanted to tell Lauren all that, but for some reason I couldn't.

So instead, I sang.

How many roads must a man walk down, before you call him a man?

I was so distracted the rest of the night—thinking about my argument with Katie—that even the s'mores, which were completely delicious, couldn't get my full attention.

I went over my entire life in my head—how I avoided the library in elementary school, and had Timmy Mc-Gibney read my books in exchange for ice cream sandwiches in middle school, and how I introduced Jake Katz to Hannah Spivero and basically watched my dream girl walk off into the sunset with my braniac friend just so he would read my books. Not to mention the fact that I had to be in the school play about paper towels, just to make sure the teacher didn't hate me.

Does that sound like the behavior of a dork-in-training? I don't think so.

Jack Strong wandered by, scraping melted marshmallow off his chin. Tonight's T-shirt said AMHERST.

"Is that another college?" I asked.

"Yeah," he replied.

"Where is it?"

"I have no idea."

"Did your dad go there, too?"

"My uncle did," Jack said. "It's a small school, but it's amazing."

I offered him my napkin. "What George said, about your dad, about how he's hyper-intense. Is that true?"

Jack thought for a second. "I guess it is," he said. "He just wants what's best for me, but yeah, sometimes he gets a little crazy."

"Have you ever tried telling him to back off a little bit?"

He looked shocked. "You're kidding, right?"

"No, I'm not kidding. If you spend too much time worrying about colleges and stuff, you won't have any time left over to just be a kid."

As Jack thought about that for a second, I looked around for Katie. I wanted her to see me in action, trying to de-nerd a human being right before her eyes. But she was nowhere to be found.

Suddenly a voice blasted from the campfire. "Yo fellow campers, wassup?!? Let's do this thing!"

I looked up. Standing in front of the fire was Jared Bumpers, the kid who wanted to be captain of the basketball team. He looked like he was about to do something obnoxious. I knew Jared's type. He was one of those kids who waits all his life to be in the oldest group, just so he could finally feel like a big deal.

Also, because Dwayne had made me captain, Jared had decided to hate me.

"So who's coming to the big game against Jockstrap tomorrow?" he hollered. Everyone kind of cheered. Jared made a face. "Louder!" Everyone kind of cheered again, at exactly the same volume as the first time.

"The team's been practicing all week," Jared went on. "We're looking good. Coach Dwayne has us ready."

No mention of Captain Charlie Joe, of course.

Then Jared looked right at Lauren. "What's your name?"

Lauren looked around, like she couldn't believe Jared was talking to her. "Lauren," she finally said.

"Well, Lauren, it's loyal campers like you that make us go out there and fight for our good name. So come up here and toast with me."

I couldn't believe what a turkey this guy was, but apparently Lauren didn't share my opinion, because she scrambled to her feet and joined Jared in front of the fire. Younger girls always fall for older guys, even at nerd camp.

Jared poured two cups of bug juice (which is camp-speak for fruit juice) and gave one to Lauren. They clinked. "Here's to the men and women of Camp Rituhbukkee," he said. "Scholars of the highest order, but also athletes and competitors. Sharp of mind and sound of body. With brain and brawn we shall be victorious!"

What was this guy talking about? I wanted to find Katie so we could roll our eyes together, but then I

So here's to the men and women of Camp Rituhbukkee.

remembered we were in a fight, so I stopped myself. Meanwhile, Lauren was staring at Jared with a "you're-awesome" look in her eyes.

Wait a second, was she falling for this guy's routine? Seriously?

Smart people are so dumb sometimes.

As I sat there watching obnoxious Jared, shaking my head at gullible Lauren, thinking about completely-wrong Katie, and wishing I was with perfect Zoe, I realized one thing.

Nareem couldn't have been more wrong. Friday Night Campfire turned out to be just another lousy thing about camp.

Dear Timmy,

How's it going? Are you having an awesome summer so far? That's good. I'm so happy for you.

The first week of camp is almost over. Tomorrow's the big basketball game with Teddy Spivero's camp. Supposedly they're amazing, and he's their best player. I'm the captain of our team, and we're horrible. It's kind of like God's playing a cruel joke on me.

But guess what? I have a plan. If it works, I'll tell you all about it. If it doesn't, pretend we never had this conversation.

Well, it's lights out. Which means all the other kids in my cabin lie there in the dark and think about the books they're reading, while I lie there and think about hanging out at the beach with you guys. Write back, if you can tear yourself away from the French fries.

Your bud,

CJJ

P.S. I haven't heard from Zoe in a while. Can you tell her to write me? Thanks.

The next day, our whole camp was waiting at the flagpole when the bus from Camp Wockajocka pulled up.

Twenty kids piled out, each one bigger than the next. The only kid we had that was as tall as them was our nineteenth-century literature scholar, George Feedleman.

"This isn't good," mumbled George, who was standing next to me.

"Don't worry, I got this," I answered.

Teddy Spivero was the last one off the bus. He spotted me right away.

"Yo, Jerko Jackson!" he hollered, pulling out one of the old nicknames. "So you're really here at Camp Be-A-Nerdie with all the dorkmeisters! Dude, you must be fitting right in!"

I felt my neck get hot with anger. It was okay for me to call my fellow campers names, but no one else could.

They may have been dorkmeisters, but they were *my* dorkmeisters.

"Good to see you, too, Teddy," I said, playing it cool. Revenge would come later. On the basketball court.

"I'm George Feedleman," said George, sticking out his hand. "I play center."

Teddy looked at George and starting guffawing. "Guys, come meet their big man!" he yelped to his teammates.

Teddy's buddies gathered around, yakking to each other and shaking George's hand. George nodded happily, not used to being fawned over by jocks, until he realized that they were actually making fun of him. Then he started blinking nervously.

Dr. Mal saw what was going on and walked over.

"Gentlemen, it's nice that we're all getting to know each other, but the Wockajocka boys have had a long bus ride, and I'm sure they'd like to stretch their legs a bit before the big game."

"Nah, we're good," Teddy offered, slapping Dr. Mal on the back like they were old buddies. "The ride was only a half an hour. Can we get something to eat, though? That'd be AWESOME."

As soon as Teddy mentioned food, Dwayne and I looked

at each other. He nodded. I nodded. The plan was in place.

"Teddy, good to see you," said Katie, who was hanging out with Nareem, as usual. "How's Hannah?"

"Probably making out with Jake as we speak," Teddy answered, elbowing me in the ribs. "Still hurts, huh?"

"Not really," I said. "It's all good. I love it here. Tons of awesome people. And unlike your camp, we have girls here."

"Do they all have hair on their legs?" Teddy asked. "Like the smarty-pants girls back home?"

I noticed Lauren Rubin and a bunch of other girls glance at their legs.

"You're such a turd," I told Teddy.

He responded by punching me on the arm and asking, "Okay seriously though, how's the talent around here? Solid? Can smart girls be pretty?"

I was in the middle of ignoring him when a completely huge, blond-haired Wockajocka kid started the Camp Wockajocka chant, and the rest of them joined in. It went something like this:

Wocka!
Wockajocka!
Wocka!
Wockajocka!
Wocka!
Wockajocka!

After about a minute, I tapped Teddy on the shoulder.

"Aren't there any more lyrics to this song?" I asked.

Teddy glared at me. "Buzz off," he snapped, chanting away while Dr. Mal led them into the dining hall for a pre-game snack.

I looked around at my fellow campers, still standing around the flagpole. They'd been completely silent the whole time. All this "Camp Jockstrap" this and "Camp Jockstrap" that, but when the other team actually showed up, no one said a word.

"Guys!" I shouted. "What gives? Please don't tell me you're scared of those clowns! Come on! They're not even smart enough to come up with a second verse to their fight song! We can take these turkeys!"

I looked at George and Jack, hoping at least they'd back me up, but they didn't. And right then I realized something. At camp, with each other, these kids felt happy, free, and relaxed. But if someone from the outside world came in, they went back to being the quiet, awkward outsiders they were the other eleven months of the year.

I grabbed Jared Bumpers by the shoulder.

"Jared, remember your pep talk from the campfire? The guys could use something like that right about now."

But Jared had lost his mojo. "Give it up, Jackson," he said. "Did you see the size of those guys? This is going to be a slaughter. Just like every year."

"No, it's not," I said.

"Stop acting like you know everything!" Jared yelled. "This is your first year at camp! You don't even belong here, so stop pretending you do."

I resisted the urge to tell him what a jerk he was being. "I'm the captain of the team," I said calmly. "And I'd like you and the rest of the team to get warmed up."

"Stuff it," Jared mumbled, but he gathered the team and started heading toward the court. I looked for Dwayne and found him over by the dining hall, talking on the phone.

"Are we all set?"

Dwayne put his hand over the phone. "Yup, all good, I'm ordering right now."

"Awesome," I said. "Who's driving Cathy?"

"I am," said Ms. Domerca, walking up behind me. "I heard about your plan. I think it's underhanded, evil, and dastardly." Then she gave me a big hug, her bracelets and necklaces smacking me in the face.

"Which is why it's completely wonderful," she added.

11

The game started out as advertised.

The huge blond Wockajocka kid, whose name turned out to be Chad, won the tip-off. The ball went to some other big kid, who passed to some other big kid, who passed to Teddy, who went in for an easy lay-up.

And so on.

The first quarter ended 18–6. Our points came from one outside shot by me, one lay-up by George, which hit the top of the backboard and bounced in, and two foul shots from Jared Bumpers. After his shots went in, Jared pranced around the court acting like he'd just slayed a dragon, while the guy he was covering went down court and scored.

"Jared, get back on defense!" I screamed.

"Don't rush me!" Jared screamed back.

Our two other starters were Sam, the kid from my cabin who could at least dribble a little bit, and a girl named Becky, who played travel basketball back home. Becky was pretty decent, but she was only four feet seven inches tall, so unless she could figure out a way to get a trampoline on the court, she wasn't going to get a lot of shots off against the Jockstrap boys.

The good news, though, was that besides Teddy and Chad, the rest of their team wasn't all that great. They were big, for sure, but it turned out they weren't really basketball players. They were more like football players who didn't realize that tackling wasn't allowed in basketball. So two of their kids got two fouls in the first quarter, which was good news, because five fouls disqualified you from the game. Dr. Mal was the referee, and some of the Wockajocka guys complained that he was calling the game too closely, but Dr. Mal wasn't about to let his campers get injured by the big jocks from down the road. I kind of liked him for that.

After the first quarter ended, we ran over to the sideline.

"Great start!" Dwayne said. (Sports expectations are different at nerd camp.) Then he took out a clipboard and started drawing Xs and Os that looked more like a tic-tac-toe game than a basketball game.

"Guys, we need to do some more pick-and-rolls," he added.

Sam raised his hand. "What's a pick-and-roll?"

Becky rolled her eyes.

"Never mind," said Dwayne. "Your job is to keep drawing fouls on these guys. If we can make some of them foul out we can win this thing."

The Wockajocka kids on the bench started a chant:

2-4-6-8

Nerdy kids can't get a date!

But our fans answered with a chant of their own.

H-I-J-K

You boys will work for us some day!

We had about fifteen minutes to go until halftime. I looked at Dwayne.

"We're all set," he said. "They're on their way back."

The second quarter started out like the first—not so good. But Dr. Mal called a couple more fouls on their guys, and I made a three-pointer (seriously, no lie), which made the crowd go wild. Teddy didn't like that, though, and made two lay-ups in a row. After the second one, he ran over to our fans and shouted, "How do you like them oranges?"

One of our writing teachers, Mr. Hodges, shook his head. "The expression is 'How do you like them apples?' " he said.

"I know that!" Teddy claimed. "I was just testing you! You people love tests, right?" He high-fived his coach, some huge guy whose knees came up to my head.

Then, about a minute before the end of the half, I had a fast break. It looked like I had an open lay-up. But out of nowhere, Teddy came sprinting down the court and blocked my shot. The ball went halfway to Antarctica. I went sprawling.

"You're in my house now!" Teddy screamed down at me. "My house!" I didn't have the energy to tell him that technically, he was in my house. I'm pretty sure he wouldn't have cared anyway.

As Teddy sauntered back down the court, I struggled to my feet. Suddenly, I heard a noise that was loud and getting louder. I couldn't quite tell what it was, but then I figured it out.

It was booing. Tons of it.

I looked over at the sidelines. Every Rituhbukkee kid was booing their lungs out at Teddy Spivero. The kids in my cabin. The counselors, too. Then they started cheering for me. "You can do it, Charlie Joe!" "Go get 'em, Jackson!" "Come on man, we're pulling for you!"

Teddy screamed at them, "Shut up! Go back to the library!" But that just made the kids boo and scream even louder.

I think that was the first time I finally felt like a true Rituhbukkean.

The half ended 34–14. On the bright side, two of the Wockajocka kids had three fouls each, which meant that two more fouls and they'd be done. But they weren't exactly shaking in their sneakers. They were ahead by twenty points against a bunch of nerds. No wonder they were laughing and high-fiving on the bench. What could possibly come between them and another Rituhbukkee humiliation?

Halftime, that's what.

Remember I mentioned a while back that I knew what Teddy's two obsessions were? I don't think I ever got the chance to tell you what they were.

Pizza, and red-headed girls.

Ever since I've known him, which is as long as I've known (loved) his sister Hannah, Teddy's favorite activities have been eating pizza and annoying me. He was able do both in our elementary school cafeteria. I would be sitting near his sister, trying to get up the nerve to talk to her, when Teddy would come over and yell, "Stop staring at my sister!" Then he'd steal my pizza and eat it in one bite. And then he'd yell "I love pizza so much!" right in my face and walk away, leaving me sitting there with no pizza, no pride, and no chance with Hannah.

Teddy discovered redheads a little after that, like around fourth grade. He started following this girl named Maureen Cochrane around, calling her "Strawberry Head." He was pretending to make fun of her but everyone knew it was a major crush. Then another girl with red hair named Kelly Gilbride moved to town, and suddenly Teddy was following *her* around too, calling her "Raspberry Head." It was definitely weird, but it wasn't creepy or anything. In fact, whenever the two girls tried to talk to Teddy, his face would turn the color of their hair, and he'd run away. I remember Katie actually saying she thought it was sweet. To this day, that was the only time I've ever heard the words *Teddy* and *sweet* in the same sentence.

But anyway, that's the story behind Teddy's two obsessions.

Which helps explain what happened next.

We were sitting on our bench during halftime when I saw the car pull up.

Dr. Mal saw it, too. "What's going on?" he asked no one in particular. "Cars aren't supposed to drive so close to the court."

But before anyone could answer him, Ms. Domerca hopped out of the driver's seat with a big smile on her face.

"Halftime refreshments!" she announced, holding about ten boxes of piping-hot pizza.

Then the passenger's side door opened and Cathy Ruddy got out, holding even more boxes.

Teddy took one glance at Cathy's fire-engine-red hair, stood up from his bench, and started staring.

She walked right over to the Wockajocka guys. By this point they were all gawking at her with their mouths wide open. Teddy's was open the widest.

"Can I interest you guys in some pizza?" Cathy said in a kind of flirty way, just like Dwayne had asked her to. "It's delicious."

Teddy and his teammates jumped off the bench and immediately mauled the pizza.

"Easy you guys, one at a time," Cathy said, which just made them eat faster.

"What's this about?" Dr. Mal asked Dwayne, in an annoyed voice. "No one said anything to me about a pizza party at halftime."

"We thought it would be a nice thing to do for the boys," said Dwayne. "The game's not that close, and who doesn't love a little pizza?"

"It might give them energy for the second half!" Ms. Domerca added.

Dr. Mal looked at them and scratched his head, like he knew something was up but didn't know exactly what. "You should have cleared it with me first. Do you have enough for all the campers, at least?"

"Absolutely," said Ms. Domerca. "Come and get it!"

As the kids swarmed around the pizza, I nodded at Cathy, which was her cue. She walked up to Teddy and put her arm on his shoulder.

"So, I hear you love pizza," she said to him.

Teddy didn't say anything. I think he was still a little scared of redheads.

Cathy tried again. "I hear it's your favorite food."

"Where'd you hear that?" Teddy was finally able to say.

"I know a lot about you," Cathy said, and smiled.

"Really?" Teddy said, feeling a little more confident. He looked right at Cathy. "Like what else?"

It was Cathy's turn to be shy. Or, at least, pretend to be. Finally she said, "Well, I heard you can eat a whole pizza in under two minutes. That is so cool."

"Totally can," Teddy said, his mouth already full. He immediately started stuffing pizza slices into his mouth.

Chad, Teddy's huge teammate, saw what was going on and came running over. "Dude, are you serious? Not smart. We have a second half to play."

"All good, bro," mumbled Teddy, tiny pieces of pepperoni spraying out of his mouth. "I got this."

Katie, Lauren, and Jack came over to me, staring at Teddy. "What is he doing?" wondered Lauren.

"It looks like he's trying to stuff a whole pizza in his mouth," I said.

"Aha," Katie said, without looking at me. She was still acting kind of mad at me from our little fight at the campfire.

I shrugged. "Aha what?"

"Aha I get it," said Katie. "The pizza. The redhead. Very good."

She knew me too well.

"What's very good?" Lauren wanted to know.

"Don't ever let Charlie Joe tell you he's not smart," Katie said.

"You don't have to worry about that," Jack said, rolling his eyes. "Charlie has never, ever, ever told us he's not smart."

"Which just proves me right," Katie said.

Jack looked confused. "About what?"

"You won't believe this," I told him. "Katie thinks I secretly wish I was a book-loving nerd like the rest of you guys. She thinks the reason I talk about hating reading so much is because I actually love it."

Jack thought for a second. "That actually makes sense," he said. "We all have secrets. I secretly wish I could spend my entire life on the couch watching TV."

"Yikes," I said. "Don't ever tell your dad that."

"I won't," Jack answered quickly.

We turned our attention back to Teddy, who had just eaten an entire pizza in about ninety-eight seconds. Cathy was clapping.

"Wow, amazing job. That's awesome," she told him, giving him her cutest smile.

"Thanks," Teddy mumbled through a jammed mouth. He was starting to sweat a lot. One of his teammates brought him some root beer. "Here, drink this," the kid said, obviously having no clue that the carbonation was going to make things worse.

Much worse.

After Teddy gulped down the soda, he wobbled over to his bench, where Chad was spinning a basketball on his finger. This was about to get good, so I went to get a closer look.

"Man, you don't look so hot," Chad said to Teddy. "I told you eating that whole pizza was dumb."

"Leave me alone," gasped Teddy. "I need to sit down."

Chad shook his head. "Come on man, we have a game to play. Are you ready to go, or what?"

Teddy paused for a minute, then answered by throwing up an entire pizza onto Chad's shorts.

Chad stared down at his uniform in shock. "Dude, SERIOUSLY?"

Teddy answered *that* by throwing up his root beer onto Chad's sneakers.

"YOU ARE SUCH AN IDIOT!" Chad screamed, as Dwayne, Dr. Mal, and the Wockajocka coach ran over to them.

"What's going on?" shouted Dr. Mal, which seemed to be his favorite phrase that day.

Chad pointed at Teddy. "This idiot just ate a whole pizza in a minute to impress some girl, and then he threw it up all over me!"

"Yeah well, I did it, didn't I?" responded Teddy, obviously feeling a little better already. "I bet *you* couldn't do it, you big oaf."

And before anyone could do anything, Chad grabbed Teddy, and they started rolling around the ground and fighting.

Not to be too gross about it, but little gobs of ex-pizza were flying everywhere.

"Eeeeew!" shouted Cathy.

Dr. Mal blew his whistle louder than I've ever heard in my life. "Get up, both of you!" he yelled at Chad and Teddy.

After a little more vomit-wrestling, they got up.

"Go get yourselves cleaned up," he said. "Then go sit on the bench. You're both out of the game."

Dwayne came over to me quietly. "Wow, this is going even better than I expected," he whispered. "We might actually win this thing."

I nodded. He was right. Operation Pizza Party had

worked out perfectly. We figured at best, we'd get Teddy too stuffed on pizza to play well. We never imagined that he'd vomit all over the other best player on the team, and that they'd both be kicked out of the game. That was truly a dream come true.

Dwayne signaled for the team to bring it in. On my way over, I grabbed Cathy.

"You were awesome," I said.

She smiled at me. "Thanks." Then she came over to the bench and gave George a kiss on the cheek.

"If you guys win," she told him, "I'll kiss you on the other cheek."

The second half was a totally different story.

After about five minutes, their third-best player fouled out, and three minutes after that, another kid did. They started to panic. All of a sudden, Becky started getting openings, and she made three three-pointers in a row. Sam made a lay-up, I made two jumpers, and George, feeling like Superman from Cathy's kiss, blocked three shots and got every rebound. Even Jared had two steals. Everyone was contributing, and we got more and more confident with each basket.

Meanwhile, Teddy sat at the end of their bench with his vomity shirt off, a towel around his head, and absolutely no appetite.

By the end of the third quarter, we were only losing 38–34.

Our fans were going wild. They could taste victory against Camp Jockstrap. For the first time ever.

"Keep it going," Dwayne told us before the fourth quarter. "They're rattled. Sports are all about momentum and confidence, and we have both right now. Let's finish it off."

Dwayne made it sound easy, but it wasn't. Their team

suddenly realized they were in danger of becoming the first team from Camp Jockstrap ever to lose to us, and they started playing a lot better. But we didn't give in, either; we kept playing hard and making shots.

It turned into a real, honest-to-goodness basketball game.

With fifteen seconds left, the game was tied 48-48. One of their kids missed a shot, and George got the rebound. Dwayne immediately called time-out.

"We're going to hold the ball for the last shot," he told us. "Who wants to take it?"

"I will," said Jared, even though he had scored only four points in the entire game.

"I want to hear from the captain," Dwayne said.

Jared's face turned red. "This is bogus," he complained, but everyone ignored him.

I thought for a second. "George should take the last shot."

George blinked and shook his head. "Absolutely not."

"No, seriously," I said. "Everybody thinks it'll be me or Becky. You'll be wide open underneath. Trust me."

George thought about it for a second, then took a deep breath. "Okay, fine. But if this doesn't go well, I'll never forgive you."

We headed back out onto the court. I took the ball out and inbounded to Becky. She dribbled up the court and passed it to Sam, who immediately passed it to me. All the Jockstrap guys swarmed around me, while George drifted down underneath the basket. I faked the shot, then snuck underneath their giant arms and threw a bounce pass to George. There were two seconds left. He looked up at the basket, mumbled something that was probably some sort of prayer, then threw up the saddest-looking lay-up I've ever seen in my life.

It rolled around the basket for about twenty minutes—okay, maybe not, but it seemed like twenty minutes—then dropped through the hoop. Everybody on both teams and in the crowd stared in silent shock for a second, until George turned around and looked at Cathy.

"It went in," he said quietly.

Then it got real loud, real fast.

People started screaming at the top of their lungs. Campers stormed the court, lifting us up on their shoulders as if we'd just won the NBA championship (or the Nobel Prize). Kids were hugging each other. Kids were hugging Dr. Mal. Dwayne got doused in Gatorade. It was a madhouse. A happy madhouse.

Meanwhile, the Wockajocka kids waited patiently to shake our hands. It turned out they were really good sports. "Congratulations, amazing game," they kept saying, over and over. Even Chad was nice about it. Teddy was the only one acting like a jerk, refusing to shake anyone's hand and not saying a word. Instead, he came over to me and stuck his finger in my chest.

"Loser," he said with a sneer. "You can't win without cheating. I know what you were up to. It won't happen this way next year, believe me. Next year we show no mercy."

I high-fived him, against his will. "Next year I'll be at the beach."

15

After the Wockajocka bus left, the whole camp went to the dining hall for a celebratory ice cream party, but it was awkward. Once the craziness at the basketball court died down, people realized they had no idea how to celebrate a victory, since it had never happened before. After a few minutes of everyone just standing around eating ice cream, Dwayne went up to the microphone.

"I have an announcement!" he said. "I just want to say thanks for coming to the game today. And I thought you might want to hear from the kid who led us to victory . . . Captain Charlie Joe Jackson!"

Everyone cheered (except Jared, of course) as I took the microphone, but for once in my life, I had no idea what to say.

"I know you guys think I hate books and learning and stuff," I said finally. I looked at Katie while I said it, since I'd recently found out she thought the opposite. "And I know it took a while to get used to me," I continued. "But it turns out I like to use my brain, too, even if it's just to figure out a way to trick a kid into eating so much pizza that he throws up."

George imitated Teddy barfing, which made everybody laugh.

"Anyway," I added, "thanks for putting up with me."

"For now," Jack added, making everybody crack up all over again.

I handed the microphone to Dr. Mal and sat down, people clapping me on the back.

"What a first week," Dr. Mal said, trying to be a good sport. I could tell he was still a little mad that he didn't know about the pizza plan, but since it was such a big moment for the camp, he decided to let it go.

"And I've got more good news," Dr. Mal continued. "Early next week I'm going to share some exciting new developments that promise to make your camp experience even richer and more rewarding."

We all looked at each other.

"What's that about?" I asked the guys, suddenly feeling a little less celebratory.

"We'll find out," said George. "I can't wait. Dr. Mal always comes through, because he's awesome."

Oh, jeez. I was definitely learning to respect Dr. Mal, but "awesome" wasn't exactly the word that came to mind.

Katie came up, and this time she actually looked at me. "Nice job," she said. But before I could decide if she was actually being nice to me, she raised her eyebrows. "Turns out it only took one week for you to feel like you belong here. If I didn't know any better, I'd say you were one of us. You know . . . a nerd?"

"Ha-ha," I said.

Katie stood there and waited.

"Fine," I admitted. "It's okay here, I guess. And the fitting in part feels pretty good. Even though I still hate books and everything associated with them."

"Wow," George said. "The idea that someone like you would feel good about fitting in with a bunch of kids like us."

"What do you mean?" I asked.

George shook his head.

"Life can be really weird sometimes," he said.

Hey Charlie Joe,

Congratulations on getting through your first week of camp. Only two more long weeks to go.

I don't want to tell you how much fun I'm having this summer because I don't want you to accuse me of secretly wanting you to be miserable, like you usually do. So I'm not going to say anything at all about how amazingly, incredibly, awesomely awesome my summer is going so far.

Seriously, I'm not going to say anything. Well, gotta go ENJOY MYSELF.

Timmy

Week Two

CAMPERS UNITE!

16

So yeah, I admit it; by the second week, I was starting to feel like I maybe slightly belonged at Camp Rituhbukkee. But there's a difference between *feeling* like you belong and *actually* belonging.

It's true, I didn't feel like a complete outsider anymore. But there were still a lot of things about camp that I just didn't get. I didn't get racing to the camp library when the new shipments of books arrived. I didn't get writing letters just for fun. And I absolutely, positively would never get reading while walking to meals.

But most of all, I still really didn't get why kids liked the classes—sorry, I mean *workshops*. Having to go to school during the summer was something I would never get used to. It's something I wouldn't wish on my worst enemy, except for maybe Teddy Spivero.

On the Monday morning after the big basketball victory, I was sitting in The Write Stuff workshop, which was the most bearable one, mainly because of Ms. Domerca. I was working on an important project: trying to get George to take his relationship with Cathy to the next level.

The kiss-on-the-lips level.

"You're a sports hero now," I told him. "That puts you in a whole new category of chick magnet."

"Would you stop?" George begged, ungratefully.

I shrugged. "Fine. She opened the door with that kiss on the cheek, is all I'm saying."

"I'm not here to date girls, I'm here to study," he insisted.

"Maybe you can study girls," Jack Strong chimed in. I laughed. Jack turned out to be pretty funny. He was still wearing his annoying T-shirts (today's said NYU), but at least he was loosening up a little.

Jack's joke turned out to be the end of the conversation. I heard the familiar rattle of bracelets, then Ms. Domerca's voice behind me.

"Sorry to interrupt, boys. Charlie Joe, may I speak with you for a moment?"

Uh-oh.

I followed her out onto the front porch of the cabin. We looked out at the big beautiful lake. You know, the one that I was currently not swimming in, because I was in a class-like workshop, in a class-like room, in a school-like building.

"What's up?" I asked.

Ms. Domerca sat on a big, rocking, bench-type thingy and started swinging back and forth. "Charlie Joe, how long have we known each other?"

Was this a trick question? "Um, a week."

"Right!" Ms. Domerca smiled at me like I'd just solved world hunger. "And in all that time, wouldn't you say that we get along pretty well, and that as teachers go, I'm not among your bottom five of all time?"

I squinted at her. "Yes, I would say that. What's this about?"

"I want you to do something for me."

I knew it. The friendliness, the compliments, the helping out on Operation Pizza Party—it was all just a trick to get me to do something.

Typical teacher maneuver.

"Like what?" I asked, expecting the worst. Which I got.

Ms. Domerca grabbed a pamphlet off of a table and handed it to me. It was a copy of the *Bukkee Bugle*, the camp newspaper.

I held it away from my body like it had some sort of dangerous odor. "Seriously?"

"Seriously. I'm the faculty advisor, and I want you to join our staff."

"Why?"

"Because I think you could be a good writer," said Ms. Domerca, smacking me on the leg. "You're funny, you're clever, and you certainly don't lack opinions. I think you'd make a fantastic addition to our team. You can be our columnist and write about whatever you want."

I raised my eyebrows. I didn't know what a columnist

was, but it sounded pretty good. Whatever I wanted? What's the catch?

"The only thing," Ms. Domerca added, "is that all your columns have to refer to a book you're reading here at camp."

There's always a catch.

"So let me get this straight," I said, joining her on the rocking swing. "I can write about whatever I want, but not really, since it has to come out of a book?"

Ms. Domerca sighed. "Why is everything such a battle with you, Charlie Joe? You have to read and write anyway. This is a camp for reading and writing. So why not try to make it as fun as possible along the way?"

I thought about that for a second.

"Also," she added, "all the kids will read it. They'll listen to what you have to say."

Hmm. That could be in-teresting. The basketball game had helped me win over some of these kids. This might get me the rest of the way there, not to mention help me in my mission to turn these nerds into former nerds.

"Fine," I agreed. "I'll give it a try."

"Great!" Ms. Domerca ran back inside. Five seconds later, she came out with a pile of books.

"I thought you'd start with these." She patted me on the head like I was a dog. "We meet Mondays, Tuesdays, and Thursdays during First Rec. The paper comes out Wednesdays and Fridays."

She left me sitting there with the books. Did I mention the books were thick? They were. Really thick. And as far as I could tell, there wasn't a single picture in any one of them.

I looked at each book for approximately no seconds, then went back inside.

"Nareem," asked George at lunch, "can you please pass the carrots?"

George liked cooked carrots, which was another thing that made him by far the least likely friend I'd ever had. Even Nareem hated cooked carrots.

"Here you go," Nareem said, as the rest of us shook our heads. Gross.

"That reminds me, Nareem," Jack asked with his mouth full, "what's up with you and Katie? Are you guys going out or what?"

Nareem looked at Jack. "How does passing the carrots remind you of me and Katie?"

"It doesn't," Jack said, and everybody laughed.

I smiled. For the first couple of days at camp, meals were used to discuss books, equations, and other tools of learning. Now, we spent most of the time talking about girls. A very significant development, if you ask me.

Nareem looked uncomfortable. "Well, as a matter a fact," he said, studying his macaroni and cheese carefully, "I have been thinking about it. I'm not sure I have time for a girlfriend right now." Then he looked at me. "What do you think, Charlie Joe?"

"About what?" I asked.

"Duh," said Nareem. "About Katie."

"I think when you two finally admit you like each other, it will make world news." I immediately realized that sounded kind of jerky, so I added, "She's like the most amazing person in the world, and it's awesome that she likes you, dude, so congratulations."

"What about you, Charlie Joe?" Jack asked. "Is there a new, nerdy girl in your life?"

"No," I said.

"What about Lauren Rubin?"

I shook my head. "Nope, just friends. Anyway, she likes Jared Bumpers, for some insane reason."

Nareem said, "What's going on with Zoe?"

"Haven't heard from her lately," I answered quickly, feeling my ears get hot. "Not since that one letter, like the third day of camp."

Nareem shook his head. "That's weird."

"Yeah, whatever." I suddenly had a burning desire to change the subject back to books and learning. "That's enough girl talk. How about that Second Workshop speed-reading exercise we did today, huh? Wasn't that a blast?"

Forks were dropped. Juice was spit out of mouths. The guys looked at each other, then at me.

"Who are you," George asked, "and what have you done with Charlie Joe Jackson?"

The coolest place at camp was probably The Table Of Contents, which was the camp canteen. Kids could go to The Table Of Contents to buy candy, soda, and other snacks, and generally hang out and have fun. The problem was that it was only open for fifteen minutes at a time, in between workshops. It was like a mini recess. Hanging out there was probably like what it feels like for people in jail when they get fifteen minutes of exercise a day.

During First Rec, The Table Of Contents became the newsroom of the *Bukkee Bugle*. The best part was, we didn't even have to pay for licorice during the meeting! Being on the camp newspaper was looking better already.

When I walked into the canteen for my first meeting, I saw a few familiar faces. Jack Strong, Lauren Rubin, and Jared Bumpers were all there.

And of course so was Ms. Domerca, in her usual way-too-good mood.

"Charlie Joe, welcome!" she sang.

"Hi," I said back.

Jack looked at me. "What's a slacker like you doing in a place of learning like this?"

I pointed at Ms. Domerca. "She asked me to come, and said I could write about whatever I want."

Ms. D. clapped her hands. "Guys, your attention for a second. Charlie Joe has joined us as a columnist. That means he will be writing opinion pieces, as opposed to doing the kind of straight reporting that the rest of you will be doing."

Jared gave me the evil eye as usual. "Wait, what? Why does he get to write what he wants?"

"The rest of you will get a chance to do opinion pieces next week," said Ms. Domerca. "We're all part of the same team."

Jared stood up. "Well, I'm going to be doing a study of campers' eating habits at breakfast, and how that affects their ability to do good work at the morning workshops," he announced. Then he put his arm around Lauren. "And I've decided to let Miss Rubin work on it with me." Lauren, who was apparently missing the part of the brain that recognized obnoxious people, nodded in agreement.

"Sounds fascinating," said Ms. Domerca, which made her the only one to feel that way. "How about someone else?" She looked at Jack Strong. "Jack, any ideas for what you'd like to write about?"

Jack sipped on a soda. "I thought maybe I'd talk to kids about how they deal with the pressure to succeed at such a young age."

"Oooh, juicy stuff," Ms. Domerca said.

"Maybe you should interview parents," I told him. "Because they're the ones stressing kids out about things like what colleges we should go to."

Jack's face got red. "You don't know anything about my parents," he said.

"Who said anything about *your* parents?" I protested, but I realized he was right. I'd crossed a line. The pressure he felt from his dad must have been intense. Being told to get good grades was one thing. Being told to get into Harvard was another.

"Sorry, dude," I told him.

Ms. Domerca turned to me. "And how about you, Charlie Joe? Have you had a chance to look through the books I gave you? Did you pick one to focus on?"

The true answer to those questions was no and no, but it didn't seem like the right time to be truthful. "Absolutely," I said. Then I reached over to the stack of books and randomly grabbed one. "I thought it would be great to read this."

"What a wonderful choice!" Ms. Domerca exclaimed. That made me curious, so I looked at the mystery book I'd chosen. There was a picture of a man on the cover. He had a big smile and a bushy mustache. Then I noticed the title. *Lech Walesa: The Road to Democracy.*

Lech Walesa? What was that? A country? A foreign language? Some kind of weird sea monster?

"Radical choice," snickered Jared with a nasty grin. "Who IS that dude?"

"It's a long story," I answered, which seemed like the safest answer at the time.

Thankfully Ms. Domerca jumped in. "Lech Walesa is one of the greatest heroes of the twentieth century," she announced. "He was a Polish worker who founded the Solidarity Movement, which was very instrumental in bringing about the fall of communism in Eastern Europe." She smiled at me. "Charlie Joe, you're in for a fascinating journey. I'm very impressed with your selection. I look forward to seeing how this book helps you craft your first piece for the newspaper. I need it by tomorrow to get in Wednesday's edition."

I tried to smile back. "Awesome."

Solidarity? Communism? Eastern Europe?

Holy moly. What had I gotten myself into?

Dear Zoe,

I'm trying to decide why you haven't written me back yet. I've narrowed it down to two possibilities: 1) your pet iguana ate the piece of paper that had my address on it, or 2) your letter got lost in the mail and wound up at some other camp with a similar name, like Camp Eataboogie.

Seriously, I'm sure you're having a fantastic and busy summer, but it would be awesome to hear back from you. Is everything okay? I got a letter from Jake that said he hadn't really seen you around much.

Right now I'm avoiding reading a book about Lech Walesa, who's famous for stopping communism and winning the Nobel Peace Prize. If you ask me, though, his greatest accomplishment is his mustache, which is awesome.

Can't wait to hear from you!

CJJ

19

"**Now's your chance,**" I said to George, elbowing him in the ribs. "Just go talk to her. Man up."

We were down at the lake during Water Sports. It was later that afternoon, and I was trying to forget all about Lech Walesa and his annoying book. I figured the best way to do it was to continue my project to help George win Cathy Ruddy's love.

George was weird about Cathy. In the cabin with the guys, he made it sound like the two of them were about to get married. But in front of her, he had a habit of forgetting how to talk.

Cathy was lying on a towel, talking to her friend Samantha, who apparently was some kind of National Spelling Bee champion.

George looked at them nervously. "Come with me," he begged me.

"Nope," I said. "It's up to you. You're ready. This is your time."

George took a deep breath, then headed over to Cathy's towel like he was walking to the principal's office. I watched as he said something that made Cathy look up and smile. They talked for a second, then George sat down. About ten seconds later, Samantha got up and ran into the water. Cathy stayed with George. Five seconds later, he put his arm around her.

I watched them, totally impressed with myself. First Jake and Hannah, now George and Cathy. If there were a college scholarship for matchmaking, I'd win it for sure.

"Charlie Joe! Charlie Joe! Charlie JOE!"

I turned around and was greeted with a blast of water in my face. After wiping my eyes, I saw Jared standing there with a bucket in his hand, cracking up. Lauren was standing next to him, looking a little embarrassed, as usual.

"Sorry, man, it just seemed like you needed to get a little wet," Jared said, still chuckling.

"You're right, I did," I said, wiping my face with a towel. "That actually felt awesome, thanks."

"No it didn't," Jared insisted.

Dwayne came marching over. "Jared, what was that about?"

"Nothing, Dwayne, just having a little fun."

Dwayne stared down at Jared. "Well, that's not the kind of fun we want to be having."

"He's sorry," Lauren interrupted.

"Just remember, free time is for relaxation, so let's all try to get along and enjoy ourselves," Dwayne said. "Especially since it might not last."

We stared at him. "What are you talking about?" I asked.

He nodded up the hill, toward Dr. Mal's cabin. "I'm hearing rumors that Doc wants to add another workshop before lunch."

Aha—so that was the "exciting announcement" Dr. Mal was talking about at the basketball celebration.

I stamped my foot, which in the sand doesn't really have any effect. "Another workshop? You can't be serious!"

"I couldn't be serious-er," Dwayne answered. "It's been in the works for a while now. Apparently the powers that be are worried that we've added too much recreation over the last couple of years, which is turning us into every other camp." He sat down on a beach chair. "Plus, I hear some of the parents have been complaining, saying that they're paying a lot of money for an academic camp, but there aren't enough academics."

We all looked at Jack, assuming his dad was the culprit.

"What?" he said, defensively.

"Leave Jack alone," Dwayne said. "It's just how the world is these days. Hyperintense and hypercompetitive."

"But this is crazy," I moaned. "We're in class all morning already!"

Katie and Nareem heard the commotion and came over. So did a bunch of other kids. The only ones who didn't seem to notice were George and Cathy, who were too busy staring at each other.

"What's going on?" Katie asked.

"Dr. Mal wants to add another workshop," I told her. "Which is perfect for me, right, Katie? I mean, since I secretly love reading and writing so much."

"Quiet, you," she said.

Nareem scratched his head. "I must say, even though I enjoy the workshops very much, I feel there's currently a perfect balance of studies and recreation."

Other kids nodded. Jeremy—the sneezer from my cabin—sneezed in agreement. "God bless you," said Nareem. He was the only one who still said "Bless you" to Jeremy. The rest of us had decided that, based on the amount of time he spent sneezing, Jeremy was already the most blessed person on the face of the earth.

Dwayne shrugged. "Dr. Mal runs the place, so if he wants more workshops, we're going to have more workshops. Or should I say, *you guys* are going to have more workshops." He chuckled. "I'll be at the basketball court, working on my jumper."

"Not cool, Dwayne," I said.

But he was already halfway up the hill. "Almost time for Quiet Hour, gentlemen," he yelled back, "and then dinner. At least Dr. Mal still lets you guys eat."

"For now," said Jack, as we trudged back to our cabin. "For now."

20

Dinner was quiet, as we all waited for the announcement we knew was coming. Our whole cabin was sitting together. George had even managed to tear himself away from Cathy. In tough times, you want to be with your buddies.

I didn't even have much appetite for dessert, for maybe the first time in my life.

Finally, the moment of truth. Dr. Mal went up to the microphone.

"Announcements. Quiet, please, for announcements." That was a totally unnecessary request, since the place was completely silent. "We have one major announcement this evening."

Dr. Mal cleared his throat. "As most of you know, we always strive to keep Camp Rituhbukkee the most satisfying, rewarding camp experience on the planet. Our mission is to prepare our campers for successful, gratifying lives."

He paused, as if he were waiting for applause, but there was none. It may have been a camp of nerds, but at a certain point, even they'd had enough.

"It is crucial that we continue to search for ways to improve our programs. We can't be afraid of change. In fact, it's essential, if we're to survive in these tough times." He cleared his throat again. "As a result, we have decided to add another academic workshop to our daily schedule. It will be called Extended Workshop, and it will discuss the application of your academic growth to the real world, in order to prepare you not just for school, but for the school of life, which can be graded very harshly."

The school of life? What a frightening thought.

But Dr. Mal wasn't done. In fact, he'd saved the worst for last. "This new workshop will meet every morning right after breakfast," he continued, "and the new schedule will result in the elimination of the 11:00 am Free Swim."

Wait, WHAT?!?!?

The entire dining room groaned, but Dr. Mal plowed ahead.

"Please. I understand your concern, but let's not rush to judgment. We will continue to have Water Sports in the afternoon. In addition, the new schedule won't take effect until Friday morning, which gives you several days to get used to the idea. Workshop assignments will be posted in the dining hall before breakfast tomorrow. That's all for tonight."

Dr. Mal put down the microphone and practically sprinted out of the dining hall. It was obvious he knew how unpopular the new plan was, and he didn't want to be anywhere near us.

If he knew what was going to end up happening, he probably would have just kept going.

Usually during the Reading Hour before bed, I did anything but read.

Sometimes I stared at the wall. Sometimes I counted Jeremy Kim's sneezes (I think the record for one hour was sixty-two). Sometimes I talked with Nareem, who was on the bunk below me, until he told me to be quiet so he could read.

But that night, after Dr. Mal's cruel and shocking announcement, Nareem didn't feel like talking, the wall didn't have any interesting stains on it, and Jeremy was too stunned to sneeze.

So I opened the book with the guy with the big mustache on it. And I started reading.

Please don't tell anybody.

Anyway, it turned out that this guy Lech Walesa wasn't a very good student and never even went to college. (I liked him right away for that.) He was an electrician in a shipyard in Poland, helping build boats I guess, until one day when he realized that the communist bosses were treating the workers really badly. So he got all the workers to go on strike until the bosses made the working conditions better. When that didn't work, he got more and more people to agree with the shipyard workers, until practically the whole country was on their side. Eventually, all the people forced out the bad bosses, which was the government, and made Lech Walesa the president of Poland.

It was a pretty amazing story, actually, even if it was in a book. When it was time for lights out, I realized I'd read like fifty pages! That's a lot, even for a human computer like George. I put the book away, but I couldn't fall asleep. I kept thinking about what this guy had done. Somehow he'd convinced a bunch of people to agree with him, to bravely fight against injustice, and they were able to do something about it.

Suddenly I sat up straight in bed. An idea hit me, an idea so simple I couldn't believe it.

I wasn't Polish, I wasn't an electrician, and I definitely didn't have a supercool mustache . . . but it was time to do my best Lech Walesa imitation.

I got out my flashlight and started writing.

The next day, at our *Bugle* staff meeting, I gave Ms. Domerca my article.

CAMPERS UNITE!
By Charlie Joe Jackson

Yesterday, Dr. Mal announced that he was adding another workshop to the morning schedule, and taking away Free Swim.

I don't think that's fair.

All of us work very hard here at Camp Rituhbukkee, especially when you compare us to our friends back home, who are hanging around at the beach or in the playground or someplace else that's fun. We're already reading and writing way more than a normal kid should have to, especially considering it's summer.

Now, we're being told that we have to work even harder. To me, that makes no sense. Just because all of the kids that go to this camp are smart, doesn't mean they want to spend twenty-four hours

*a day doing schoolwork-type activities. No one
likes reading THAT much.*

*So what are we campers going to do about it? I
have an idea.*

I have been reading the book Lech Walesa:
The Road to Democracy, *which is all about how
people who unite together can tell the people who
are in charge of them that they're being unfair, and
if they stick together they can make those people
stop being unfair.*

That's what I propose we campers do.

*Let's stick together. Let's refuse to go to this
extra workshop! Let's demand more fun activities!*

*In the words of Lech Walesa, "We have the right
to decide our own affairs, to mold our own future."
I agree! Campers unite!*

*The new workshop is supposed to start on
Friday. We have two days, my fellow campers. It's
now or never.*

✳ ✳ ✳

Ms. Domerca read it without saying a word. Once
in a while, she nodded, but that was about it.

After she finished, she still didn't say anything for
about a minute.

Eventually she looked up at me. "*Unite together* is re-dundant," she said. "When people unite, they're together by definition."

"Okay," I said. "That's it? Anything else?"

Another long pause. Then she sighed and shook her head.

"It's excellent," she said finally. "It runs tomorrow."

Dear Hannah,

Camp is almost half over, which is very exciting!

But that means camp is only half over, which is very annoying.

How's your summer going? Please tell Jake I say hi, and then immediately break up with him. Also, tell Zoe to write me back.

See you soon,

Charlie Joe

George Feedleman was a great kid, but he'd developed this annoying habit of combing his hair for, like, ten minutes every morning. He wasn't the most handsome guy in the world, to be honest with you, but he was really proud of his hair. Way too proud.

On Wednesday morning, he was taking even longer than usual, and the rest of us were starting to get impatient.

"Dude, you're hogging the mirror," I said. "You look great. Move it along."

George ignored me.

"Come on," I said.

"Make up your mind, Charlie Joe," George said, still staring at himself. "You're the one who told me there was more to life than studying. That I should get out there and get a girlfriend and live a little. Well, guess what? I'm living." He gave his reflection a thumbs-up. "And if you don't mind, I prefer to do my living with excellent hair."

I looked at this guy, who'd spent his entire life being the school dork. Now all of a sudden he was acting like he was the man. All because he was going out with Cathy Ruddy—thanks to me, by the way. (Have I mentioned before that I set them up?)

"Well, whatever," I said. "Cathy doesn't like you because of your hair."

"She likes you *despite* your hair," said Jack, who was sporting a T-shirt that didn't say a college, for once. It said NORTHRUP DISTRICT YOUTH ORCHESTRA, which was almost as bad.

"What do you know about hair?" Nareem asked Jack.

"What do you know about girls?" Jack asked him back.

"A lot more than you," Nareem responded.

"So you're the big expert now?" answered Jack.

Nareem ended the conversation by snapping his towel at Jack.

Jack re-started the conversation by smearing toothpaste on Nareem's underwear.

"Cut it out!" Nareem hollered.

There was a bang on the wall. "Would you kindergartners give it a rest for once?" Dwayne yelled. I think it was the first time Dwayne had ever yelled at anyone besides me.

I was so proud of them.

Dwayne came into the main room. "Jackson."

I put down my Lech Walesa book, which for some reason I was taking a quick look at before breakfast. "What's up?"

"I got a call this morning. Dr. Mal wants to see you in his office after breakfast."

"What about?"

Dwayne shrugged. "I don't know, but getting summoned by the big man is never a good thing."

George wandered in, looking like Justin Bieber's nerdy cousin.

"What's up, Charlie Joe?"

"Don't know. Mal wants to see me."

George put his various hair items back in his trunk. "Well, I'll come with you. No one goes to see Dr. Mal alone."

Kenny Sarcofsky, who never said anything unless it was to talk about the healing powers of garlic, nodded and said, "I'll come, too."

The rest of the guys all nodded their heads, too.

"We'll all go," said Nareem.

"Totally," said Jack.

I shook my head. "Nah, I got this."

I wasn't sure I had anything, to tell you the truth. Except the guys in the cabin. I knew I had them.

It was a good feeling.

24

At breakfast, I noticed three things right away.

The first was the copy of the *Bukkee Bugle* that sat on top of everyone's plates.

The second was that the dining room was a lot quieter than usual.

And the third thing was the reason for the silence. Everyone was reading my article, which was at the top of the front page.

George was reading it with his mouth open.

When he finished, he said one word.

"Wow."

"Wow, what?" I asked him.

"Wow, this is awesome."

"Thanks."

He shook his head. "You've got nerve, Charlie Joe, I'll give you that much."

I was starting to thank him when I felt a tap on my shoulder. I looked up to see Dwayne smiling down at me, holding a copy of the paper.

"Dang," was all he said, then he walked away.

He was just the first. During the entire breakfast, kids and counselors came up to me in a steady stream, saying one of two things: I was awesome or I was crazy. Sometimes both.

Katie was one of the last to come talk to me.

"I really liked your article," she said.

"Thanks."

"See you later."

"See ya."

I watched her walk back to her table, and kept watching as she said something to Nareem. Then he laughed, she smiled, and he put his arm around her shoulder.

Just like a real couple.

✱✱✱

"Announcements!"

Dr. Mal's shorts were shorter than ever as he took the podium.

"Today after lunch, there will be a meeting to help prepare the study materials for our Overnight Adventure next week to Old Bridgetown and the Little Yellow Schoolhouse. Anyone who's interested please meet at Workshop Cabin 3, where Dr. Kretzler will be supervising."

Kids started murmuring excitedly. I'd already heard something about the Overnight Adventure, which was supposedly the big event during the last weekend of camp. Everyone talked about it like it was this awesome thing, but I wasn't sure how a trip to a school could be awesome. It kind of sounded like the opposite.

"Also," continued Dr. Mal, "we're very much looking forward to our first morning of Extended Workshop, which you'll remember is in two days."

The room got very quiet.

Dr. Mal looked around the room, then stared at me. "This is something that we've been planning for a long time, and I have no doubt that once our new schedule is up and running, it will be just the latest in a long line of wonderful changes that have helped make Camp Rituhbukkee the preeminent academic camp in America."

He stopped. All the kids turned and looked at me, as if they expected me to get up and lead a protest, but I couldn't do it. It's one thing to write an article. It's another thing to stand up to the camp director in person.

You would need to be Lech Walesa to do that.

Dr. Mal's office was on the top floor of the dining hall. Climbing the stairs behind him, I felt nervous, but I tried to look on the bright side—I was missing First Workshop.

When we got to his room, I was surprised to see Ms. Domerca sitting there.

"Have a seat," Dr. Mal said to me, pointing at a chair.

I sat.

He sat down, too. Then he leaned back in his chair and twirled his pen for about a minute. Finally he sat straight up and stared at me.

"I love students like you, Charlie Joe," he said. "I really do. I admire your intellectuality, curiosity, and independent thinking. It's the first step toward leading a fulfilling life."

He stopped, and I waited. Surely he didn't call me in here to compliment me on my "intellectuality," whatever that was.

"Here's the thing, though," he continued. "This camp has an advisory board, with over three hundred years of combined experience in education. Your parents pay us to make thorough and thoughtful decisions, which benefit the welfare of the children. You have to trust me on this one.

The decision to create Extended Workshop was not something we took lightly, and I would appreciate your support."

I didn't want to look at Dr. Mal, so I looked over his head and at the wall, where there were about six thousand diplomas from six thousand colleges in six thousand frames.

"What do you mean by 'support'?" I asked.

"Well," said Dr. Mal, "it would be great if for Friday's edition of the newspaper you wrote an article about how you're willing to give Extended Workshop a chance, before passing judgment on it."

I looked at Ms. Domerca. "Is that what you want me to do?"

"Ms. Domerca and I have discussed it," said Dr. Mal before she could answer. She looked at her feet, and suddenly I felt bad for her. I figured she probably got in trouble for picking up the pizzas at the basketball game, and I'm sure Dr. Mal didn't love the fact that she published my column. She wasn't really in a situation to argue with him about anything.

I took a deep breath and looked at Ms. D again. She nodded a little sadly.

"Okay," I said to Dr. Mal.

Dr. Mal jumped out of his chair and shook my hand. "Good news, Charlie Joe. I really appreciate your flexibility on this one. That's just terrific. If you hurry, you can still make the rest of First Workshop."

We were heading out the door when we both realized that Ms. Domerca was still sitting in her chair.

"Are you coming?" Dr. Mal asked her.

She sat there for a second, then slowly shook her head. "Actually, no. Something doesn't feel quite right about this."

Dr. Mal stared at her. "I'm sorry?"

Ms. Domerca got up and stared at the same wall I had, with all the framed diplomas. "You're a brilliant man, Malcolm," she said. "Surely you understand how important it is to endorse freedom of expression in our students. And how dangerous it would be to try to censor them, at this impressionable time."

"That's not the point," said Dr. Mal.

"I think it *is* the point," said Ms. Domerca. "I'm ashamed at myself for almost going along with this. Charlie Joe, you write whatever you want. And frankly, I think you make a very good point. I'm not convinced we need this extra workshop." She turned to look at Dr. Mal. "I think the kids at this

I think it IS the point!

120

camp—kids like Jared Bumpers, who's trying to live up to his brother's brilliance, and Jack Strong, who's spent his entire middle school career molding himself into the perfect college applicant—could use a little more swimming and splashing and running and jumping and just general fun."

She strode toward the door. "Now if you gentlemen will excuse me, I'm late. Charlie Joe, I'll see you in Third Workshop."

And she left.

Dr. Mal slowly sat back down in his chair, staring into space.

"Um, I'm gonna go," I said. And I walked out, leaving him sitting there with a very annoyed look on his face.

Dr. Mal might have six thousand diplomas, but I was pretty sure he just got schooled.

Dear Charlie Joe,

Thanks for writing! I hope you're doing okay! I know that you're not exactly loving camp, and I feel bad for you. But maybe by the time you get this, things will be a little better, and anyway, it will be almost time for you to come home. Everyone will be very happy to see you, especially me!

Jake and I were talking about maybe throwing a welcome-home party for you, Katie, and Nareem. Do you think that would be fun? Speaking of Katie and Nareem, I got a letter from her that said she and Nareem were kind of going out! Is that really true? That is so cool! You must be so psyched for them!

Can't wait to see you!!

Xoxo,
Hannah xx

The next day, I got to The Table of Contents a little early. The only person there was Lauren, who was already working on her story.

"Hey, Lauren," I said. "Where's Jared?"

She smiled self-consciously. "He'll be here in a minute, for sure. Our story is due today."

That was typical. After watching the two of them for a few days, I'd noticed a pattern: Lauren was the one who did all the work, and Jared was the one who took all the credit.

"Cool," I said, sitting down next to her.

Lauren looked up from the computer. "I thought your article yesterday was awesome," she said. "Really brave."

"Wow, thanks."

"You're welcome."

After another second, I asked her, "So, do you like Jared? I mean, *like* like him?"

Another self-conscious smile. "He's pretty cool, I guess." She looked at me, as if she were waiting for me to tell her I thought he was a jerk, but I couldn't do it. This was probably exciting and new for her, being liked by a boy— especially an older boy—and who was I to ruin it for her?

"That's great," I said. "You must be totally psyched."

"I guess." Then, as if she was trying to convince herself, she added, "He's really cool once you get to know him."

"Awesome," I said, trying to sound like I meant it.

The door opened with a slam. "Speak of the devil," Lauren said, as Jared, Jack, and a bunch of other kids piled into the room.

"Lauren and I have been working on our piece and it's really coming together," Jared announced to nobody in particular. "Sweetie, want to grab it?"

The rest of us all looked at each other. *Sweetie?*

Lauren handed Jared the article she'd been working on, and he cleared his throat. "As most of you know, we're doing an article about camp food. So far, we've interviewed the head cook and two of his assistants, and the results have been fascinating."

I was trying to figure out how to not listen to the rest of their report when the door to the canteen opened again. I turned around, thinking it was Ms. Domerca, but in walked Dr. Singer instead. Dr. Singer was a pretty old guy who'd been the camp director before Dr. Mal, and he still had an office at camp. As far as I could tell, he mostly walked around and looked over people's shoulders while they were doing stuff. Some people called him "The Breather," because when he was hovering over you, his breathing was pretty distracting. So was his breath, which always smelled like cough syrup.

But he was an okay guy, so we were all perfectly happy to see him. Especially me, because his arrival meant the end of Jared's report on camp food.

"Hey, Dr. Singer," I said. "If you're looking for Ms. Domerca, she's not here yet."

"Which is weird," said Jack, "because she's never late."

Dr. Singer sat down and sighed, sending cough syrup fumes across the room. "Well, that's why I'm here, children." (He always called campers "children.") "Unfortunately, Ms. Domerca is no longer able to be the staff supervisor for the camp newspaper. I'll be taking over for the rest of the session."

We all looked at each other. No one knew what to say. Or, more accurately, they expected me to say it.

I stood up. "Is this because of my article yesterday, and our meeting with Dr. Mal?"

Dr. Singer shook his head. "She has other responsibilities she needs to attend to, which makes her unavailable for this activity. I'm afraid that's all I know." He nodded at Jared. "I believe you were reading from your piece when I walked in. Would you like to continue?"

"Sure," said Jared. "As I was saying, we've interviewed all three cooks—"

"Hold on a second," interrupted Jack. His voice sounded a little nervous. "Ms. Domerca would never just quit the camp newspaper. She loves working on it, and she loves working with us. This doesn't make any sense."

"That's true," agreed Lauren. Everyone else nodded. Jared was the only one who didn't seem to care too much one way or the other, as long as he got his food article in the next day's paper.

"I understand how you all feel," said Dr. Singer. "She's a wonderful teacher, and it hurts to lose her. But as all journalists know, the newspaper comes first. So let's concentrate on getting tomorrow's edition out the door."

"Dr. Singer's right," I said suddenly. "Let's get tomorrow's newspaper done. I know I have an article due, and Jared and Lauren have the food thing, and Jack has his stress article. Let's finish this issue. We have some important things to say, and the camp is counting on us. Ms. Domerca wouldn't want it any other way."

Lauren and I looked at each other, and we both nodded. Everybody seemed to understand what I was trying to say: The best way to fight for Ms. Domerca was in the newspaper itself.

Dr. Singer clapped his hands together. "That's what I like to hear! I'll be outside, if anyone needs me or has any questions." He took a book out of his bag, went out to a couch on the porch, and promptly fell asleep.

The rest of us all looked at each other.

"Let's get to work," I said.

27

Later that day, after the intense meeting at the *Bugle*, I was really looking forward to getting on the basketball court. Dwayne claimed the court was still a little wet from the rain the night before, though, and we weren't allowed to play.

"Dude!" I begged. "Come on!"

Dwayne answered by telling me not to call him "dude." Then he asked me if I wanted to be dunked like a basketball. I said no.

"Don't worry, little man," he said. "I've got an even better game planned."

Uh-oh. Dwayne had a talent for coming up with the most exhausting drills ever invented by man.

"What kind of game?" asked Nareem.

"This is going to be awesome," Dwayne said, which meant that it would be the opposite of awesome. "I want you guys to each take a ball and dribble down to the tennis court and back."

We all groaned. The tennis court was on the opposite end of camp.

"And because this is a camp of learning," Dwayne went on, winking, "I want you to count how many

128

dribbles it takes to get there. Assuming you can count that high."

We all groaned louder.

"You've got to be kidding," moaned Jack, who was wearing an unfortunate T-shirt that said SMART IS THE NEW COOL. (Which just proved that it wasn't.)

"This is a reading and writing camp," complained Nareem, "not a math camp."

"Same thing," Dwayne said. Then he looked at me and laughed. "If you guys think it's unfair, you can always get Charlie Joe here to write an article about it."

"Ha-ha," I said.

As we set off on our journey, Nareem came up along-side me. "Charlie Joe, thank you again for your advice about Katie. As you may know, we are now officially going out, and it's wonderful."

"I didn't know, but that's great," I answered. "Twenty-two . . . twenty-three . . . twenty-four . . . ."

Nareem wasn't finished. "Naturally, I would be happier if you two would resume your normal friendship."

I kept counting.

Jared was eavesdropping, as usual. "Are you still mad at Katie for calling you a secret nerd?" he asked, getting too close to me. "I don't know why you don't just admit it, Jackson. She's right. You're totally trying to become like the rest of us. You're even writing for the camp newspaper now, which is pretty much page one of the nerd handbook. Look it up."

"I don't read handbooks," I answered. "Or any other kind of books, for that matter."

"You do now," Jared said.

"Leave Charlie Joe alone," said George, distractedly. It was taking all of his concentration to avoid bouncing the ball off his foot.

Seven hundred and forty-eight dribbles later, we got to the tennis courts, where a big crowd was gathered.

"Oh right, today's the camp tournament!" exclaimed George. "Girls' final!" He was right. I suddenly realized Dwayne was actually giving us a break by sending us down here to let us watch the tennis match. (That's the thing about Dwayne: if you ignored his I-will-break-your-body approach to life, he was a really good guy.)

As we got closer, I noticed who was playing: Katie Friedman and Cathy Ruddy. Or as they're otherwise known, Nareem's girlfriend and George's girlfriend.

I wasn't totally thrilled to see Katie, to be honest with you. It's not like we were fighting, exactly, but Nareem was right: things were off between us. We weren't relaxed around each other, which was different for us.

Different as in, it had never happened before in our entire lives.

The match went back and forth. Katie and Cathy were both pretty decent, for a couple of bookworms. I tried not to care, but it was a close match, and I ended up paying close attention. Finally, Katie won. The crowd whooped and cheered as the two girls hugged, then came off the court.

When they saw George and Nareem, they came running over. All four of them said "Hi!" to each other at the exact same time.

"What are you guys doing here?" asked Katie.

"Yeah, don't you have basketball?" added Cathy.

"Dwayne let us come watch," said George. "You guys are really good, by the way."

"Really good," agreed Nareem.

"Not really," said Cathy, "but thanks."

"Yeah, thanks," said Katie.

"No problem," said George.

Then they all just started smiling at each other.

"I hate to break up this incredibly fascinating conversation," I said, "but we should go."

Katie looked at me. "Charlie Joe, what is WITH you?"

I shrugged. "What?"

Her eyes flashed with anger. "You can do the most interesting things—like your article yesterday, which was actually pretty brave—and yet you're capable of being the biggest jerk!"

"How am I being a jerk?"

Katie looked shocked at the dumbness of my question. "Well, for one thing, the whole camp came and cheered for you at the basketball game against Camp Jockstrap, but when we're playing in the tennis tournament finals, you act like you'd rather be anywhere else."

"That's so not true," I said, even though it was.

Katie shook her head sadly. "You're being mean to me for absolutely no good reason."

"You were mean to me first."

"No I wasn't."

Nareem threw up his hands. "Would you two stop this nonsense right now!" he demanded. Katie and I stopped the nonsense, right then.

Nareem looked at us. "You two have been best friends your whole lives," he said. "And now you're acting like kindergarteners, for the silliest reason in the world."

"Being called a nerd is not silly," I insisted. "It's a matter of life and death."

"I never said you were a nerd!" Katie yelled. "I said you were a smart person who wanted to learn! How is that so horrible?"

I thought for a second. "Because you're calling me a phony."

Katie's face changed, as if she'd been slapped.

"I would never call you a phony," she said finally.

Nareem stepped in again. "Think about it, Charlie Joe. Katie is your biggest fan. She thinks you're hilarious and smart and you're basically her best friend. How could she possibly think you're a phony?"

I had no answer to that one.

George tried next. "I think what Katie's really saying, Charlie Joe, is that maybe you're realizing there's more to life than trying to avoid reading books. There are a lot of interesting things and people in the world that are worth learning about, and reading about. Is that possible?"

I thought about that for a second.

"Not really," I said.

Katie sighed. "You're unbelievable. Are you ever going to grow up?"

I smiled. "Hopefully not. Listen, I hate to ruin the fun, but we need to get back, or Dwayne is going to make us dribble around the whole rest of the camp backwards."

"That would not go well," Jack said.

We all headed off except for George and Nareem, who lingered behind. George hugged Cathy, and Nareem hugged Katie. Then they kept hugging.

"Let's go, you guys," I called to them. "Seriously."

As George and Nareem finally tore themselves away, Katie stared at me with her hands on her hips.

"What?" I said. "You guys could hug until Christmas, for all I care. It's Dwayne who'd be mad, not me."

Katie rolled her eyes, just like the way she did when we were six years old and I'd told her that books could kill you. That eye-roll always made me laugh. I looked at her, and for a split second I wanted to tell her that I thought she was the funniest, coolest person in the world.

Instead, I just said, "Congratulations on your victory," and walked away.

28

That night, after lights out, I wasn't tired, and I couldn't stop thinking about Katie calling me mean.

So I borrowed Sam's flashlight and read some more of the Lech Walesa biography.

It was only because everyone else was asleep and I had absolutely nothing else to do.

I swear.

29

Friday morning, when people walked into breakfast, they saw copies of the *Bugle* on each plate, which was normal.

They also saw a note on top of each copy, which was not at all normal.

> *From the Staff of the*
> Bukkee Bugle:

> *We're sorry to announce that this will be the last edition of the* Bugle *for this summer. Both of next week's issues, including Friday's special Overnight Adventure Preview, have been canceled.*
>
> *We cannot stand by after our staff supervisor, Ms. Domerca, was taken off the newspaper for defending the right of one of our reporters, Charlie Joe Jackson, to express his opinion.*
>
> *Therefore, we are all resigning our positions at the paper, effective immediately.*
>
> *We hope you enjoy this last issue, which includes the long-awaited analysis of camper eating habits as they affect academic productivity*

—written by Jared Bumpers and Lauren Rubin—as well as an article about kids and stress, by Jack Strong.

Sincerely,
The Staff of the Bukkee Bugle

We'd come up with the idea for the staff note Thursday afternoon, while Dr. Singer was snoring away on the couch. Lauren wrote most of it. Jared made us put in the phrase *long-awaited*. It was a small price to pay for a unanimous vote.

When Dr. Singer woke up, we showed him the final issue—without our secret addition, of course—while a girl named Becky Esposito quietly printed out copies of the note in the back room. Dr. Singer had no idea what we were up to, poor guy.

Then, just before breakfast, Jack and I put the papers and the notes on each plate. Dr. Mal didn't realize what we'd done until he sat down at his own table, thirty seconds before the campers walked in.

By then, it was too late.

I watched him as he read the note. The top of his bald head turned red, and he snapped his neck around— looking for me, probably. He didn't find me, but he did find Dr. Singer, who was reading the note at his own table. The two of them looked at each other and hurried out of the dining hall, probably to decide what to do.

That's when I made my move.

I went to the front of the dining hall and grabbed the microphone. I was as nervous as I've ever been in my life. But then I thought of Ms. Domerca, and how unfairly she'd been treated. I took a deep breath and started talking.

"Announcements, please! Announcements!"

The room fell completely silent.

"Okay, I know I'm not Dr. Mal," I continued. "And I know it's the beginning of the meal, not the end. But I have an important announcement."

I saw Dr. Mal and Dr. Singer heading back into the dining hall. I figured I had about fourteen seconds.

"Today is supposed to be the first day of Extra Workshop, but I say it doesn't have to be. For anyone who wants to skip it and go for a swim instead, please head down to the lake right after breakfast."

The two doctors were about six seconds away. I raised my fist. "As Lech Walesa once said, 'Our firm conviction is that ours is a just cause. We hold our heads high, despite the price we will pay.'"

Dr. Singer grabbed the microphone out of my hand. Dr. Mal took my arm and steered me out of the room.

"Freedom is priceless!" I shouted back toward the campers.

I heard the applause begin as the door shut behind me.

I think Lech would have been proud.

On our way to his office, Dr. Mal told me he was calling my parents.

"I should warn you, this may well result in us sending you home," he said.

A sudden image of the beach flashed through my head. Unfortunately, it was immediately followed by an image of me grounded for the rest of the summer.

"I don't want to leave."

"We'll see."

Dr. Mal dialed my home phone number and waited, while I prayed that my mom answered and not my dad. It was a weekday morning, so my odds were good, even though Dad took some Fridays off in the summer.

After a few rings, someone picked up. "Mrs. Jackson?" asked Dr. Mal.

Prayers answered.

"I'm very sorry to call you like this, but we have a bit of a problem," Dr. Mal told her. "Charlie Joe has insisted on breaking a few rules here at camp in our first few weeks. Last week he ordered pizza in the middle of a basketball game, and now he's asking children to skip one of our workshops and go swimming." He paused for a minute, no

141

doubt listening to my mother tell him how deeply embarrassed she was. "Well, no, I'm not sure yet, but I think it's best if the two of you talk about it first, for a brief minute."

Dr. Mal held out the phone. I looked at it like it was a piece of celery, but eventually I took it.

"Hi, Mom."

She started right in. "Seriously, Charlie Joe? You can't make it through three weeks at summer camp without getting into major trouble?"

She was angry, frustrated, and yelling. But here's the weird thing: I was still happy to hear her voice.

"I'm sorry, Mom, I didn't do anything that bad. Last week we actually beat Teddy Spivero's camp in basketball, and this week I was just expressing my freedom of speech."

My mom paused in shock. "Freedom of speech? What do you know about freedom of speech?"

"Lech Walesa, this Polish guy in this book, is all about freedom of speech. And Ms. Domerca, the teacher, she got taken off the camp newspaper because she stood up for me."

She sighed. "Put Dr. Malstrom back on the phone."

I handed the phone back to Dr. Mal. "She wants to talk to you."

He took the phone and listened. After a second he said, "No, he doesn't seem to want to leave." Another pause. "I know. I'm surprised, too." And another pause (Mom certainly had a lot to say). "I can't say that I have," said Dr. Mal, answering some question that was probably along the lines of, have you ever had a kid who was such a nightmare in the entire history of your camp?

"The board will meet this afternoon and make a final decision," Dr. Mal told my mom. "I can tell you, though, we don't have a lot of wiggle room with this kind of behavior."

He looked at me like he couldn't wait to get rid of me, and I started thinking about what I would do for the rest of the summer if I were locked in my room.

There was a knock on the door. Dr. Mal held his hand over the phone. "Who is it?"

"Marge." Marge Shockey was the director of water sports. She was tall and freckled, and her skin always had that wrinkly, prune-ish look of someone who's been in a bath for seven hours.

"What is it, Marge?" Dr. Mal called.

Mrs. Shockey came in, looking a little nervous. I don't think she'd spent a lot of time in Dr. Mal's office. In fact, I'd probably been there more than she had, by that point.

"Sorry to interrupt, but I thought you should know that something's happening down at the lake."

"Damn it," Dr. Mal said, breaking his own very strict no-swearing rule. He returned to the phone. "Mrs. Jackson, we're going to have to call you back in a bit." He turned to Mrs. Shockey. "What are you saying?"

"Kids are starting to show up asking to take a swim."

The top of Dr. Mal's bald head turned redder than a tomato. "Exactly which kids?"

Mrs. Shockey swallowed deeply before she managed to croak it out.

"Well," she said, "pretty much the whole camp."

Dr. Mal, Mrs. Shockey, and I ran down to the waterfront, and sure enough, kids were hanging around the dock in bathing suits, laughing and fooling around and definitely *not* on their way to Extra Workshop. (Ms. Domerca was there, too, talking to the kids from the *Bugle*. She was wearing a purple, pink, and orange bathing suit that had peace signs and flowers all over it, which turned out to be a perfect look for her.)

I couldn't believe everyone had actually shown up. It was just like Lech Walesa said. *We have the right to decide our own affairs and mold our own future . . . and he who puts out his hand to stop the wheel of history will have his fingers crushed.*

Dwayne came up to Dr. Mal. "I couldn't stop them, Boss. At first a few kids started coming down, and I made them turn around. But then they all started coming, and there wasn't anything I could do."

"Thank you, Dwayne," said Dr. Mal. "I'll take it from here."

Dr. Mal put his hands up, and everyone fell silent. Campers were revolutionaries only up to a point, I guess.

"Can I ask why everyone is down here at the lake,"

Dr. Mal asked, "instead of at the first session of Extra Workshop?"

No one moved. A few people looked at me, waiting for me to say something, but I'd just been in Dr. Mal's office talking to my angry mother, and I wasn't in the mood to be all that talkative right then.

"If no one has anything to say," Dr. Mal went on, "I'd like everyone to return to their cabins, please get changed and report for workshop. That's enough of this nonsense. We're already twenty minutes behind schedule."

People started shuffling around, not sure what to do next, then started slowly heading away from the water. I looked around, wondering if this was the end of the line. The shortest revolution on record. Ten minutes.

I wanted to shout, "Stop! Swim! Don't listen to him!"— which would have been kind of an awesome rhyming cheer, now that I think about it—but I just couldn't. I wasn't quite as brave as Lech Walesa, it turned out. Probably because I didn't have the mustache.

Then someone said, "I'd like to say something."

It was Katie.

Everyone stopped as she stepped up to the front of the dock. She wasn't wearing a bathing suit, by the way. Just regular shorts and a tank top. Katie was never big on swimming.

"Dr. Mal," she began, "I think this camp is amazing and that you're a fantastic camp director. I love it here, and I can't wait to come back next year, and maybe even eventually become a counselor."

He looked down at her, smiling just a bit. "Thank you, Katie."

"But," she added, "I don't think that in this instance you're being fair."

Dr. Mal stopped smiling.

"In his completely inappropriate way, Charlie Joe is making a pretty good point," Katie went on. "We all work really hard here. But this camp isn't all about work. It's about play, too. I think what makes it so great is that it has just the right balance of work and fun."

"She's right," Jack agreed, nervously staring at the sand. "We kind of like it the way it is. You can only work so much."

I couldn't believe it. The most dedicated kid at camp, stepping up! I hoped his dad would never find out about what he'd just said.

Other kids murmured their agreement. Maybe the revolution wasn't over after all.

"But Dr. Mal has a point, too," Katie added, looking at me. "We're here to learn, because we love to learn. And we should take every advantage of the opportunity, since we're only here for three weeks."

"That's true, too," said someone else. Soon everyone was chattering away about the ups and downs of Extra Workshop.

Dr. Mal wasn't sure what to do. He was used to being a dictator. But there was no way he could argue with Katie, whom everybody respected, and who had just told him how great the camp was. Finally, he said, "So, Katie. What do you suggest?"

"Well," she said, "it just so happens that a bunch of us have been thinking about it, and we have an idea." She nodded at Nareem, who cleared his throat.

"What if we have Free Swim today?" he suggested. "Then next week, we have Extra Workshop Monday, Wednesday, and Friday, and Free Swim Tuesday and Thursday?"

Dr. Mal hesitated and looked around, as if searching for advice that never came. "I'll need to discuss it with the board."

George stepped up, looking scared but determined. "With all due respect, sir, we don't want to wait for the board's decision. We, the campers, think this is a fair compromise. We would like to be treated with respect, and have you honor our suggestion."

He looked at Cathy for support. She nodded. "Otherwise," he went on, "we will not report to Extra Workshop at all."

George stepped back, and everyone clapped him on the back. I couldn't believe it. My fellow campers—the kids I thought were hopeless, comically challenged dorks just two weeks ago—were totally stepping up.

I was proud to call them my friends.

Dr. Mal took out his cell phone and made a phone call that lasted approximately thirteen seconds. He put his phone away, looked up at the sky, then back down at Katie.

"Deal," he said.

Everyone burst into cheers so loud the ducks flew from the lake.

But if Dr. Mal thought that he was done making deals, he was wrong. Lauren was the next to walk up to the camp director. "Dr. Mal," she said, "we would also like to have Ms. Domerca back as our staff supervisor at the *Bukkee Bugle*."

"I'm glad you brought that up," Dr. Mal told Lauren. Then he walked up to Ms. Domerca. "I'm sure we will be able to work something out. I regret that whole incident.

You should always be free to express your opinion here, without fear of reprisal."

"I appreciate that, Malcolm," said Ms. D. She looked at me and winked.

Wow, I thought to myself. This seemed like it was heading for a happy ending!

"And you have to compromise too, Charlie Joe," Katie said.

Why is it that happy endings always have a catch?

"Compromise how?"

Katie put her arm on my shoulder. "Think about where your ideas came from, Charlie Joe. How you came up with this whole camper-strike thing. How you found out about the hero you were trying to be like. And your idea for the inspirational speech at breakfast this morning. Where did all that come from?"

I removed her arm from my shoulder. "What's the compromise already?"

She grinned. "You have to say out loud to the whole camp that reading isn't the most horrible, awful thing in the whole entire universe."

"WHAT?"

"And that books can actually be quite wonderful and valuable."

All eyes were suddenly on me. I froze. I think it probably would have been easier for me to run naked through the dining hall at dinnertime.

She elbowed me in the ribs. "Come on, Charlie Joe, say it."

"Yeah, say it," Jack said.

"Just say it," Lauren added.

"Actually, I'd like to hear it as well," Ms. Domerca chimed in.

While I was trying to figure out what to do, Dr. Mal walked up to me. "I remember your first day at camp very well, Charlie Joe," he said. "You proudly announced that you'd never read a book from cover to cover in your entire life. Well, from what I understand, you recently read a book on Lech Walesa, and that's why we're here, at the waterfront, instead of at our new workshop." He stood over me, his big, bald head blocking the sun, just like on that first day at the Welcome Ring. "So surely this must help you realize the value and importance of books."

I thought for a second. Katie wouldn't leave me alone until I gave her some small victory. And Dr. Mal, for all his love of reading and learning, wasn't such a bad guy after all, and he'd had a tough day.

I figured why not give them each a break, just this once.

"Okay fine," I said as softly as the human voice can go. "Reading isn't the most horrible, awful thing in the entire universe."

"Go on," Katie said. "A little bit louder this time, please."

I looked for a hole to crawl into, couldn't find one, then took a deep breath and closed my eyes.

"And sometimes books can be quite wonderful and valuable," I said.

All the kids gasped sarcastically. Then they roared. Even Dr. Mal cheered.

Someone yelled, "Charlie Joe read a book!" Soon, the entire camp was chanting, *"Hey hey, ho ho! A book was read by Charlie Joe!"*

I wasn't done. I wanted to add that reading one book doesn't make someone a nerd. But I decided to let it go. Katie had saved my skin, so the least I could do was let her think she was right, that I really was a book lover at heart. I'd have plenty of time to correct her later—as in, the whole rest of the summer, when I wouldn't read anything. Not even a menu.

I went over to her.

"Thanks," I said.

We hugged.

"For nothing," I added, and ducked before she could smack me.

As kids started jumping into the water to enjoy Free Swim, Dr. Mal and Ms. Domerca came up to me.

Dr. Mal spoke first. "Charlie Joe, we'll make a Rituhbukkean out of you yet. Even if it kills me. Which it may well. I'll go call your mother and tell her you'll be staying." Then he headed up the hill, shaking his head.

Ms. Domerca watched him go, then put her arm around me.

"Oh, Charlie Joe," she said.

"Oh, Ms. Domerca." I waited for her to thank me for helping get her back on the paper, and congratulate me for being a hero. But instead she just looked me straight in the eye.

"Next issue of the *Bugle* comes out on Wednesday," she said. "Got any ideas?"

Week Three

THE LITTLE YELLOW SCHOOLHOUSE

33

Poke. Poke.

"Charlie Joe."

Poke. Poke.

"I need to tell you something."

Poke. Poke.

"I'm ready to learn how to kiss a girl."

I was lying on my bunk, face to the wall, trying to decide whether or not I was happy or sad that there was only one more week of camp left. Life can be so confusing sometimes. Especially when someone is poking you in the back.

Poke. Poke.

"C'mon, Charlie Joe, you're the only one here who knows how to kiss. You need to teach me!"

I flipped over and saw George staring at me, his glasses foggy with sweat.

I turned back to the wall. "Not now, George."

Jack looked up from one of the college test-prep books he read for fun. "Help the guy out, Charlie Joe. If only so the rest of us don't have to listen to his whining."

I groaned and got up. I didn't want to talk about kissing. Kissing reminded me of the two girls I'd actually kissed: Hannah Spivero, the world's most perfect creature, who was now going out with Jake Katz, and Zoe Alvarez, the world's other most perfect creature, who hadn't written me back in a week and a half.

"I'm not really in a kissing mood right now," I told George.

George looked puzzled. "I'm not actually asking you to kiss me."

"I knew that," I said quickly. "So, what then?"

George took off his glasses and cleaned them, which was something he did whenever he got nervous.

"Well, things are going really well with Cathy, and I'm pretty sure she likes me."

"Duh," I snorted. "You really are Einstein." (I know that sounds mean, but he could take it, since he basically *was* Einstein.)

"Charlie Joe, you don't understand," George said. "I've never been liked by a girl before. It took me a while to get used to the idea."

He was right, I didn't understand. I'd been liked by Eliza Collins, the prettiest girl in school, for about five years straight. Too bad I didn't like her back.

"I'm still not sure how I can help," I told George. "It's not like I've kissed a thousand girls." Nine hundred and ninety-eight less, to be exact, but he didn't need to know that.

"Well, here's the thing," George said. "Friday is the Overnight Adventure. I thought that might be the perfect time to make my move. You know, before camp ends."

Overnight Adventure, just to remind you, was not a fun trip to an amusement park or a beach. Sure, that's what a typical camp would do, but since when were we a typical camp? Nope, we were going to Old Bridgetown, which was one of those fake towns that are set up just like olden times. Not only that, we would be spending most of our time at the Little Yellow Schoolhouse, which was supposedly one of the oldest schools in the country. Yay, right? But wait, there's more. We'd be camping out in tents, which was cool, but instead of telling ghost stories and roasting marshmallows, we were supposed to build a campfire and listen to Dr. Mal give a speech about the schoolhouse, because THERE WAS GOING TO BE A TEST ABOUT IT THE NEXT DAY.

I know, I couldn't believe it, either. What a treat.

Anyway, back to George, who wasn't about to give up. "So, how do you make your first move?" he asked. "What's the first stage of the kissing process?"

Only at Camp Rituhbukkee would someone ask about the "first stage of the kissing process."

"Okay, fine," I said. "I've got one word of advice for you, and that's it."

Suddenly all the kids were at my bunk, listening. Apparently I was not only the best basketball player at camp, I was also the best kisser. Meaning, I was probably the only kisser.

I paused, to let the suspense build.

"What is it already?" asked George, getting impatient.

"Yeah, what's the one word?" Jack wanted to know. "Is it tongue?"

We all stared at him.

"What?" Jack said. "I happen to know the tongue is a very important part of kissing."

"Ew," said Jeremy, speaking for pretty much the entire cabin.

I sat down, ready to offer my word of wisdom. Everyone leaned forward. Then I waited a second more, just to torture them a little bit.

"Gum," I announced, at last.

Everyone leaned back. George scratched his head. "Gum?"

"Yup, gum," I said. "Here's the crazy thing about kissing: You're thinking about so many things before you do it, that when the time finally comes, you can't remember anything. Your mind goes totally blank. So if I gave you some advice like 'put your hand on the back of her neck' or something, you'd totally forget to do it until it was too late, then you'd do it at the wrong time and it would be stupid."

Everyone thought about that for a second.

"But gum is easy to remember," I continued. "That's why gum is the key. Because bad breath is a deal-breaker. And everyone gets bad breath when they get nervous. Your throat gets itchy, and your mouth gets dry, and your breath gets real gross, real fast."

George nodded, like I'd just proved the theory of relativity.

"Gum," he repeated, committing it to memory in that incredibly powerful brain of his.

"Not just any gum," I clarified. "Bubble gum. And make sure you give her a piece."

George blinked through his glasses. "Why's that?"

"Because watching a girl blow bubbles is hot," I said.

Everyone cracked up. "Bubbles are hot!" Jack said, guffawing. "That's the craziest thing I ever heard!"

Suddenly Nareem, who had been the only one not hanging on my every word, decided to add his opinion.

"It's true," he confirmed. "Bubbles are very hot."

I pictured Nareem blowing a bubble. Then I pictured Katie blowing a bubble. Then I pictured Katie kissing Nareem. Then I decided I didn't want to think about kissing anymore.

"Can we talk about something else?" I asked, but the rest of the guys were too busy laughing about kissing and blowing bubbles to even hear me.

As the last week of camp wound down, three interesting things happened:

1) The Free Swim/Extended Workshop compromise worked really well, and Dr. Mal started acting nice to me.
2) I read a pretty decent book about Greek mythology, but I made sure to hide it whenever Katie was around.
3) George started chewing a lot of bubble gum.

35

The day before the Overnight Adventure, there was another end-of-camp tradition: the campers vs. staff basketball game.

Dwayne called me over before the game. "I named Jared Bumpers captain of the kids' team for this game."

I made a face.

"Listen, I get it," Dwayne said. "But he's older, and this is his last year as a camper. It's the right thing to do."

"Fine."

Jared's first official act as captain was to not start me. "I want you coming off the bench, to give us a spark," he said.

I looked at Dwayne, who laughed. "Take one for the team," he said.

When the game started, George was on fire. I think all that bubble gum gave him superpowers. That, plus the fact that besides Dwayne, the staff was just as unathletic as the campers. Either way, when I went into the game in the second quarter, we were already winning, 14–8, and George had ten points.

I was guarding Ms. Domerca. She'd never really played basketball before, so I didn't have a lot to do. But what she lacked in skill, she made up for in trash talk.

"Hey, Jackson, watch this move and learn a thing or two."

"Charlie Joe, are you sure you belong on the same court with me?"

"Get ready to be taken to school, rookie."

She kept up a steady stream of chatter until the middle of the third quarter, when I went around her and sank a pretty sweet reverse lay-up. She immediately high-fived me. When her teammates reminded her that I was on the other team, she smacked her forehead and said, "Oops! I can't believe I did that! Charlie Joe, I totally take that high-five back." Then she winked at me and whispered, "Not really."

Did I mention that Ms. Domerca was pretty awesome?

In the fourth quarter, Jared got even more annoying. He started showing off to Lauren, by hoisting shots from all over the court. None of them went in. Meanwhile, Lauren cheered every time he managed to dribble the ball without kicking it out of bounds. Their developing relationship was one of the great mysteries of camp. Why did Jared, who thought he was the coolest guy around, decide to like Lauren, one of the quietest girls at camp? And why did Lauren, who was a really great person, decide to like Jared, who wasn't? And for that matter, how could a wonky brainiac like George suddenly be all about kissing and chewing gum and blowing bubbles and making shots like a superjock?

I guess when it came right down to it, the answer was simple.

Camp does strange things to people.

With two minutes to go, we were ahead 30-26 (not exactly a high-scoring battle). Suddenly a car pulled up to the court, just like during the Camp Jockstrap game.

This time it was Dr. Mal who got out.

"Pizza!" he yelled.

"Pizza!" the campers yelled back.

Dr. Mal, Dr. Singer, and Ms. Domerca started handing out slices of plain, pepperoni, and pineapple pizza to the entire camp, with cartons of apple juice to wash it down.

When Dr. Mal handed me my slice, he said, "It's not basketball without a pizza party, right, Charlie Joe?"

That may have been Dr. Mal's first funny joke of the entire summer.

We didn't even bother finishing the game. As we walked off the court, Ms. Domerca came up to me. "Rematch next summer," she said. "And your butt will be mine."

"We'll see," I laughed.

And that was the moment I realized something was different.

Had I just talked about the idea of possibly coming back to camp next year, without saying "over my dead body" at the end of the sentence?

Camp does strange things to people, indeed.

36

Friday morning before breakfast,
Dr. Mal went up to the microphone. "Announcements,
please. Announcements."

We looked up, surprised. Usually he made announcements after meals. Was something wrong? Or even
better, was something right? Was the Overnight Adventure canceled?

No such luck.

"Right after breakfast, we'll be going back down to our
cabins to pack up, then we head to the buses at eight o' clock
sharp. It takes approximately two hours to get there." Dr.
Mal pointed at Dwayne. "Dwayne, who is the supervi-
sory counselor on this O.A., has put a copy of today's
schedule on each table."

I took a look. It wasn't pretty.

Dr. Mal gave us a minute to let the schedule sink in,
then added, "Tomorrow morning, of course, we will return
to the Little Yellow Schoolhouse at eight a.m. for the two-
hour Final Workshop, before heading back to camp."

He was back in his seat before anyone could ask any
questions. Like for example, why were we only going to
Ye Olde Fudge Factory for fifteen minutes? What's with

OVERNIGHT ADVENTURE SCHEDULE	
10 AM arrival	*Set up the campsite*
11 AM	*Snack*
11:45 AM	*Head back to the buses*
12 noon	*Arrive at Old Bridgetown*
12:15 PM	*Tour the village*
1 PM	*Lunch*
2–4 PM	*Workshop at the Little Yellow Schoolhouse*
4:15 PM	*Visit Ye Olde Fudge Factory*
4:30 PM	*Buses*
5 PM	*Rest hour in the tents*
6 PM	*Dinner*
7 PM	*Campfire*
9 PM	*Lights out*

the *Ye Olde* part, anyway? And why bother calling it "Final Workshop" when everyone knows it's really a two-hour test, just as annoying as the kind you have in school, only longer?

"Overnight Torture is more like it," I mumbled. "I can't believe this."

George looked at me and laughed. "Just remember what Lech Walesa once said about dealing with adversity."

"What's that?"

"I believe the exact translation," George said, "is 'tough noogies.'"

We sang arias on the bus ride to Old Bridgetown.

You don't know what an aria is? Neither did I.

Turns out they're songs from operas, and they're not even in English. But Ms. Domerca LOVES 'em. So she made us sing something from some opera called *La Bohème*, which is French for "Holy moly, this is boring."

"Whatever happened to 'Old Macdonald Had A Farm?'" said Jack, who was sitting next to me in a T-shirt that said READ A BOOK, JUST FOR THE FUN OF IT! (Not possible, fyi.)

"*Ee-i-ee-i-o!*" I sang. "Now those are lyrics I can relate to."

Jack laughed, as usual. He always laughed at my jokes.

"So, Charlie Joe," he said. "What's the deal? Any chance you're coming back next year?"

"I don't know, dude. I would have to say probably not," I told him. "You guys are awesome and everything, but I'm more into hanging out at the beach and eating ice cream than sitting in classrooms. It's just who I am."

"Right," Jack said, looking a little disappointed.

"You really love it here that much?"

"Well, yeah," he said. "I do love it here. I love coming here." He stared out the window. "Getting away from home is definitely part of it. I mean, my dad does get a little crazy sometimes, but my parents are basically pretty cool, my grandmother who lives with us is awesome—"

"And so are her cookies," I interrupted.

"Yeah, and so are her cookies," Jack agreed, smiling. Then his face got a little sad. "But I don't have that many friends back home. Everyone thinks I'm kind of a dork. And I can't really disagree with them. At camp, though, everyone is kind of like me, and that makes it really fun." He turned and looked at me. "You wouldn't get it."

"What do you mean?"

"Come on," he said. "When you get home, you'll get to do whatever you want, and hang out with your friends and stuff. Not me. I'll start right back in with cello lessons, and a science internship, and karate, and Chinese classes."

"You do all that? In the summer?"

"That's nothing, you should see the school year."

"Wow," I said. "That's insane."

"I know," Jack agreed. "It's kind of insane."

"But what about what you said at the Camp Jockstrap game?" I asked him. "When you said that secretly, you wished you could spend your entire life sitting on the couch watching TV and stuff."

Jack laughed. "Like that could ever happen."

"Dude, you're just a kid!" I said, practically yelling at him. "You don't have to do *anything* if you don't want to.

Just tell your parents that you're tired of being so busy. Take a stand."

He smiled a little sadly. "You mean like Lech Walesa? And Charlie Joe Jackson?"

"Yup!" I smacked him on the back. "Exactly! You could do it, seriously." I pointed at his T-shirt. "And you could start by getting some new clothes."

He looked down at his shirt. "Yeah, I suppose."

We were interrupted by Mrs. Domerca, who clapped her hands loudly right behind our heads.

"I can't hear you two! Come on now, sing!"

I looked up at her. "Can we sing 'Bingo' next?"

"Oh, I love that one," said Jack. "B-I-N-G-O!"

"Please?" I asked Ms. D. "Pretty, pretty, pretty please?"

She threw up her hands. "Fine," she said, "but first things

first." She dropped a letter in my lap. "Last mail call of the year!"

I looked at the handwriting and my heart skipped about four beats.

Finally.

Jack leaned over. "Is it from Zoe?"

"Yup."

"It must be so cool to get a letter from a girl."

I took a deep breath. "I'll let you know in about thirty seconds."

Dear Charlie Joe:

I'm sorry for not writing sooner. I guess I was nervous or something, but that's no excuse really. Like I said, I'm sorry.

I don't know if you heard from anyone else, but I'm moving back to my dad's house this week. My parents are getting back together, if you can believe it. We'll see what happens. Anyway, I wanted to tell you before you got back home and I was gone.

I'll only be a couple of hours away, so I really hope we can still be friends and see each other and hang out, if you want to. Let me know.

I hope you're having a great time at camp, even though it's all about reading and writing and studying and stuff. If I know you, you'll figure out a way to have fun anyway.

I miss you.

xox
Zoe

38

I read the letter in about five seconds, then re-read it about fifty-five times.

So it was official: Zoe Alvarez would not become my first real girlfriend ever.

The girl who taught me how to stand up for myself, and how to stick things out when they weren't going so great, was moving away.

I was really looking forward to seeing her after camp ended, and hanging out with her at school, and maybe going out with her for real.

And now that wasn't going to happen.

* * *

Sitting there on the bus, I started to get mad. I wished I'd gotten kicked out of camp after all. Then I'd be home, and even if I'd been grounded I could have snuck out of the house and gone to see Zoe at least once before she moved away. But instead, I was stuck on this bus, heading to some annoying schoolhouse in the middle of nowhere. By the time I got home from camp, Zoe would be gone. And "a couple of hours away" might as well be "on the moon." I'd probably never see her again.

But then, the more I thought about it, the more I started to change my mind.

I realized that maybe it was a good thing that I went to camp. If I'd been home, I might have started to like Zoe more and more, and then it would have been even worse when she moved. And instead of hanging around the same old people at home, I made some new friends. Obviously I would never, ever, EVER become a big book lover like Katie predicted, but I'd actually discovered one or two that weren't terrible. And I found out that I could go to the strangest place on earth and still figure out a way to fit in.

So yeah, by the time we pulled into the campsite, I'd decided that Camp Rituhbukkee was the greatest place on earth, and that going to camp was the best decision I'd ever made. And I was going to prove it to the world—and Zoe—by paying attention at Final Workshop and nailing the test!

Rule number one about love: Finding out that the girl you like is moving away can really do strange things to a guy's brain.

The campsite was pretty cool. We set up our tents in the woods, with a huge fire pit right by the lake. Afterward, we ate a delicious snack of peanut butter crackers, popcorn, and juice—three of my favorite things. It was like Dr. Mal had heard I'd decided to love camp and wanted to help convince me I'd made the right decision.

Then we piled back on the buses and drove to Old Bridgetown, which was much less convincing.

Everything looked as if it were from Revolutionary times. There were a bunch of little houses where shoemakers were making shoes, glassblowers were making bowls, and blacksmiths were making whatever it is that blacksmiths make. People were walking around in those really uncomfortable-looking costumes, which made me have a quick, scary flashback to last year, when I had to dress up like Byron Chillingsworth, the famous English boy fox hunter. (Long story.)

Anyway, I'm not exactly a huge fan of these kinds of places. People are way too friendly, and there's no cable TV. And I'm not all that interested in how people had to read by candlelight. (Seems like a lot of extra effort, if you ask me.) But whatever. The point is, I was a little creeped out, and we hadn't even gotten to the Little Yellow Schoolhouse yet.

Then I saw Ye Olde Fudge Factory.

It was glorious.

Zoe's moving away became a distant memory, at least for a little while, as I ran to the store and immediately began drooling. It was full of the most delicious-looking fudge I'd ever seen in my life. And all sorts of flavors, too—regular fudge, peppermint fudge, peanut butter fudge, white chocolate fudge. I wanted to try every last one of them. But that's not all; they had more than just fudge. *Way* more. Rows of caramel apples, peanut brittle, chocolate-covered raisins, almond bark, and more of my favorite kinds of candy. Plus, big barrels full of penny candy, like Mary Janes, root beer sticks, and rock candy.

Have I gone on long enough about Ye Olde Fudge Factory?

I was staring, with my tongue somewhere around my shoelaces, when I felt a hand on my shoulder. I turned around.

Ms. Domerca.

"Gotta go," she said. "Lunch."

I ignored her and turned back to the window of happiness. Ms. D. let me stare for two more seconds, then gently steered me away.

"We're coming back later," she promised.

"For fifteen minutes," I reminded her. "That's just so wrong. We should think about reversing the schedule; spend fifteen minutes at the schoolhouse, and two hours at Ye Olde Fudge Factory. That's how normal American people do it."

Ms. Domerca sighed. "Charlie Joe, that attitude is exactly what's wrong with this country. Too much eating, and not enough reading."

Oh, Ms. Domerca. Will you never learn?

40

"**Children,** my name is Schoolmistress Prudence Moffitt. Please have a seat."

Schoolmistress Moffitt, whose real name was probably Sheila Johnson or something like that, was standing at the front of a really old-looking wooden schoolroom, which was the entire Little Yellow Schoolhouse. She was wearing a huge blue skirt that puffed up at the bottom and a white hat that was pulled tightly around her face. I hoped she was getting paid a lot of money to wear that outfit, but I doubted it.

We all sat in our usual places: Nareem next to Katie, George next to Cathy, and Jared next to Lauren. The three happy couples of camp, together for two more days.

Except for Nareem and Katie, of course, who'd be together for the whole next school year. How nice for them.

I sat quietly at a tiny desk, with a strange-looking book and an even stranger-looking pen in front of me. Hopefully no one would notice that I was actually paying attention. I hadn't told anyone about my plan to ace the test. I wanted it to be a nice, big surprise.

"Children who sat in desks like these were the lucky ones," Schoolmistress Moffitt said. "They were from homes wealthy enough to afford schooling. Many children in the seventeen-hundreds were working in the fields and farms and couldn't go to school. In the early colonies, children's literacy rates were only seventy-five percent."

"I totally would love to be one of the twenty-five percent," said George, cracking everyone up.

"Stop trying to imitate Charlie Joe," Jared told him. "You love reading. That's why you're here."

"Mind your own business," George said, turning red.

"Knock it off," Dr. Mal said. "Both of you."

As they knocked it off, I thought about the weirdness of what had just happened. George Feedleman—the kid who was too scared to even utter one word during Ms. Domerca's workshop way back on the first day of camp—was being yelled at for making jokes about not reading. Meanwhile, I was sitting there like an angel, trying to get a perfect grade on a test.

Things had sure changed.

"As I was saying," Schoolmistress Moffitt continued, "children attending school were the lucky ones. What you see in front of you is the kind of book they wrote in, called 'copybooks,' because paper was so expensive. The pens are called 'quills,' which were dipped in ink. Go ahead and try it. Write your name on the first page."

I dipped my quill in the ink, then wrote *Charlie Joe Jackson* on the first page. It actually looked more like **CHARLIE JOE JACKSON**. It was hard to write with that quill thing, but it was pretty cool.

Then Dr. Mal stood up in front of the class.

"For the next two hours," he said, "Schoolmistress Moffitt will take us on a wonderful reading tour of the books, speeches, and other writings of the Revolutionary War period. Tomorrow morning, for our Final Workshop, you will answer a forty-question worksheet on what we've learned today and then compose your own essays in the writing style of the time. The topic of the essay will be, 'The most important thing I've learned at camp this session.' This essay will conclude our workshop schedule for the summer. I'm very proud of all of you." He smiled. "And now, I leave you in the good hands of Headmistress Moffitt. Have a wonderful workshop!"

As Dr. Mal walked out of the room, I thought I saw him nod at me.

Just in case, I nodded back.

✳ ✳ ✳

Two hours later, I'd learned everything about how hard it was to live in 1770. I was ready for that test.

But first, it was time to take advantage of one of life's modern conveniences.

During our absurdly short, fifteen-minute visit to Ye Olde Fudge Factory, I asked the guy who worked there, whose name was Bart, how he got the job.

"I just applied."

I was shocked. "You didn't have to go to fudge school, or do some intense training program or anything? They just took you?"

"Yup," said Bart. "It's not that hard to make fudge. You can learn in like three hours."

I took an extra-large piece of a free sample and smiled to myself.

From now on, when anybody asked me that annoying question of what I wanted to be when I grew up, I'd finally have an answer.

41

The weather was perfect for the campfire. It had been really hot and humid most of the summer, but that night was kind of cool, with a nice breeze. The most amazing thing was that there were no mosquitoes, even though we were by a lake. The tents were up, the sleeping bags were out, and the marshmallows were ready to go. Everything was just right.

But sometimes, the only problem with "just right" is that it makes you think of the one thing that would make it even righter.

Zoe. Moving-away Zoe.

I guess that's why I was feeling a little weird when Katie came over and sat down next to me at the fire. I hadn't really seen her all day, busy as I was with the quills and the copybooks and the memorizing of seventeenth-century farming techniques. But I'd seen her with Nareem a few times. They were holding hands, in a way that kind of looked like they'd been holding hands forever.

I would even go so far as to say they were experts at holding hands.

I tried to give Katie my friendliest smile. "Hey!"

"Can I talk to you?"

"Sure, what's up?"

She hesitated for a second, then said, "I just wanted to say that I think it's great how well you've done at camp. I'm really proud of you."

"Cool," I said. I appreciated what she'd said, but I wasn't feeling very talkative.

"I know I tease you, Charlie Joe," Katie said. "And maybe even sometimes I get you a little mad. But that's only because we've known each other for so long that I feel like I can say anything to you. I hope you know that."

I nodded.

"Nareem might be my boyfriend," she added, "but you're my oldest friend."

"Thanks for saying that."

"And I hope you feel like you can say anything to me, anytime," Katie continued. "It's more important than anything in the world that we're honest with each other."

"I totally agree," I said.

"Okay, good," Katie said, but she didn't seem satisfied. She was looking at me like the therapist she would probably become one day.

I sighed. "What?"

"Do you?" Katie asked. "Do you feel you can say anything to me? Because if you didn't, I don't know what I would do."

"What are you asking me, Katie?" Thoughts of Zoe and Katie and Hannah got all jumbled up in my mind, and I started to get that annoyed feeling again. "Is there something you think I'm not telling you? I *am* always honest with you. Like when you accused me of secretly wanting to be a nerd, I was completely honest when I told you that was the dumbest thing I ever heard in my life."

"I'm not talking about that," Katie said, sounding a little annoyed herself. "If you really want to know . . . I just want to make sure you're not upset with Nareem and me for going out. Especially now that we're about to go home and head into the rest of the summer and the school year and stuff."

Ahhh, so *that* was where this was headed.

"I'm totally cool with it!" I insisted. "Why wouldn't I be cool with it? I'm totally cool with it!"

Katie shrugged. "Well, I don't know, you've acted kind of weird about it all summer. I just wanted to make sure you weren't jealous, I guess."

Wow. There it was. She'd said it.

The *J*-word.

I thought for a minute, trying to figure out what to say.

Part of me wanted to tell her that maybe she was right, that maybe in some weird way I *was* a little jealous, not to mention a little irritated that she and Nareem took forever to decide to become boyfriend and girlfriend, which combined with the fact that she thought I secretly wanted to be a nerd, made me act a little bit like a jerk sometimes, and I was really sorry.

And another part of me wanted to tell her that by the way, I just found out Zoe was moving away, and even though I was trying to make the best of it, maybe this wasn't the best time for her and Nareem to be all lovey-dovey all the time, right in front of me.

But instead, I just said, "Like I already told Nareem, I think it's awesome that you two like each other. Seriously, I'm totally happy for you!"

Katie looked at me like she was trying to decide if she believed me or not.

"Besides," I added for some reason, "I've never liked you that way, you know that."

I thought I saw a flicker of disappointment flash across Katie's face, but I might have imagined it.

"Great!" she said, hugging me.

I kind of hugged her back.

"Great!" she said again. "I'm so happy!"

I wasn't sure if she meant she was happy because of me, or because of Nareem.

I decided not to ask.

So the drama between me and Katie was over, at least for now.

But the excitement at the campfire was just beginning.

After my fun little chat with Katie, I walked around looking for a marshmallow to roast, when I ran smack into Lauren Rubin.

"I've been looking all over for you," she said.

She was crying.

"Lauren, what's the matter?" I said, as we walked down to the lake. "What is it?"

"I've been an idiot."

"That's not possible," I said. There were definitely no idiots at Camp Rituhbukkee. Nerds, yes. Idiots, no.

"Trust me, I have. This whole thing has turned out to be a complete joke."

"What whole thing?"

Lauren tried to dry her tears, but they were just replaced by new ones. "The Jared thing."

"What Jared thing?"

"He's a jerk." Lauren sat down on a bench and started throwing rocks into the lake. I watched her, but didn't say anything. I just waited for her to be ready to explain what she meant. Finally she turned back to me.

"Jared was just pretending to like me all summer so I'd do all his work for him."

I stared at her. "Holy moly. Seriously?"

Lauren nodded. "Seriously. This whole time I've been helping him with his work. Helping write a lot of his papers. I think that's the only reason he's been hanging around with me."

Even I wouldn't have thought Jared could stoop that low. "That's insane," I said.

"Insane but true," Lauren said. "It turns out he actually hates reading and writing."

I had to sit down to take that one in.

OMG. Jared sounded like me.

Which might have been the most upsetting news I'd ever gotten.

"So then what's he doing at Rituhbukkee?" I asked.

"Good question," Lauren said, sniffling. "I guess his older brother went here and he's some kind of genius, or something like that, and so Jared feels a lot of pressure to be like his brother."

Wow. First Jack feels the heat from his dad, and now Jared tries to be like his brother. Being a nerd was definitely waaaaay too stressful. But you know what? Jack handled his stress way better than Jared, if you ask me.

Lauren kept talking. "And I was so excited that he liked me that I didn't even care. Then earlier tonight, we're talking about tomorrow's Final Workshop, and he tells me we have to sit next to each other. 'What do you mean,' I said, 'we always sit together.' Then he says no, it's more than that. I have to sit on his left side and make sure I don't put my arm over my paper. I ask why and he says, 'So I can copy your answers, duh!' Then he laughs, like it's the most obvious thing in the world."

She zinged a rock at a tree. It nailed the bark with a loud THWACK! "I should have known," she said.

"I can't believe it," I said. "What a cheater. I always knew

there was something about that kid." I started skipping my own rocks. "What are you going to do?"

"What *can* I do?" Lauren wondered. "I guess I'll let him copy my answers. If I don't, he'll probably hate me forever."

"Absolutely not," I said immediately. "If you let him copy your paper, then you're cheating, too. You could get thrown out of camp forever."

(You're probably wondering why a guy like me, who has other kids read my books, is suddenly so concerned about cheating; but hey, Lauren was a better person than me, so why should she stoop to my level?)

"But I'm too scared to tell him!" Lauren cried. "He'll kill me!"

"Good point," I said. "Can I ask you something though? Why you're telling all this to me? Why not, like, Katie?"

"I don't know," Lauren said. "I just thought maybe . . . you'd know what to do."

"Oh."

Okay. Lauren had a problem, and out of all the brainiacs in camp, she came to me. That was pretty cool. "Well, we'll have to come up with a plan," I said.

"Like what?" she said, looking at me hopefully.

"Let me think for a minute."

I thought for a minute . . . then for another minute . . . and then for another minute . . .

And then it hit me.

A good plan. Actually, a perfect plan. A plan that had only one weakness.

It would get me banished from Camp Rituhbukkee forever and hated by everyone who went there. And just when I decided I liked camp after all!

I know: It was a pretty big weakness.

But when I looked at Lauren sitting there crying, I realized I had to go for it.

"I have an idea."

"What's that?"

"If you're not at the test, Jared can't copy your answers."

"Why in the world would I miss the test?"

I picked up a rock that was perfectly flat and tossed it. It skipped six times.

"Because I'm going to miss the test, too," I said.

The next morning, Lauren sat next to me on the bus to Old Bridgetown.

"Are you sure about this?" she asked.

"Very," I said. "Just remember to wait for my signal. Where's Jared?"

"I've been avoiding him," she said.

"Good."

"Also, I've been thinking . . ." Lauren added.

"Uh-oh," I replied. "That's your first mistake."

She tried to smile. "What if we get caught? I don't want to get in trouble for Jared, he's not worth it."

I laughed. "Well, you won't, but *I* will."

"Well then, I don't want YOU to get in trouble!"

"That's okay," I told her, "I'm used to it."

She sighed. "I've never done anything like this before. It's not exactly being honest."

"No one has to know," I answered. "Ever."

Lauren still looked unsure.

"Your only other option," I continued, "is to go tell Dr. Mal right now about what Jared wants you to do."

"I can't do that," she said quietly. I wasn't sure if that was because some tiny part of her still wanted to protect

193

Jared, or because she was so embarrassed that she ever fell for him in the first place.

Maybe both.

* * *

The bus pulled into the Old Bridgetown parking lot— the only part of the whole place that didn't look like it was from the 1700s—and we all piled off. As soon as we started walking to the Little Yellow Schoolhouse, I doubled over and grabbed my stomach.

"I don't think that sausage agreed with me," I said to Dwayne. "I need to make a quick trip to the bathroom."

Dwayne looked at me like he didn't quite believe

me—can you imagine?—then finally nodded. "Fine, hurry up," he said.

I went over to the bathroom and shut the door. After a few minutes, I snuck around to the back of the schoolhouse, where I hid behind a tree for five more minutes. Then I crept up to an open window and listened.

Two minutes later I heard Dr. Mal's voice.

"I thought you said he went to the bathroom!"

Dwayne replied, "That's what he told me. I went to find him and he was gone."

A hand slammed down on a desk. "This kid is killing me," Dr. Mal said. "Killing me!"

Then the schoolmistress's voice: "How would you like to proceed?"

"We're already running behind," Dr. Mal told her. "Let's get started. We have to head back to camp by ten o'clock."

It was time. I threw a small pebble against the window.

That was Lauren's cue.

Five seconds later, I heard her voice. "I think I might know what happened. Last night at the campfire he told me he would probably do badly at Final Workshop, and his parents would be so mad they'd make him take summer school when he got home. He was kind of panicky and didn't know what to do."

I heard some rustling—maybe people moving around, to hear Lauren better—then her voice again: "He said the same thing on the bus ride here this morning. He said he would rather run away and skip the test, then take it and do really badly. He said he was going to sneak off and go somewhere. I didn't think he was serious, or I would have told you."

Dr. Mal: "Sneak off where?"

Schoolmistress Moffitt, forging ahead: "Students, please begin."

Lauren: "He did mention a place, I think."

Dwayne: "He did?!?"

Dr. Mal: "He did?!?"

Both: "WHERE?!?!?"

Lauren, sounding very flustered (she was a good actress): "I don't know! I mean I'm not sure!"

Dr. Mal: "It's okay, it's not your fault. Let's calm down, everybody. Lauren, do you think you can remember?"

Lauren: "He did mention someplace, but I was focused on the test and it was loud on the bus and he was whispering and I wasn't really listening. I'm really sorry."

"It's okay," said Dr. Mal again.

"I think if I saw it I'd remember, though." Lauren added. "Maybe someone could take me around Old Bridgetown. I think if I saw the name of the place I might remember."

Next I heard whispering, and then finally Dr. Mal's voice: "Fine. Dwayne will walk the grounds with Lauren. I'll stay here with the other campers, in case Charlie Joe comes to his senses and returns."

The plan was working perfectly, but then I got a special treat. I heard Jared say, "Seriously? Why does she get out of taking the test? That's so not fair."

"This doesn't concern you, Jared," said Dr. Mal, which made Jared moan and groan for another minute. It was awesome.

Sadly, though, I couldn't stick around to hear any more whining, because I had to get to Ye Olde Fudge Factory, and fast. I figured I had about five minutes to get there—enough time for Lauren and Dwayne to walk around Old Bridgetown, and for her to "realize" it was the Fudge Factory she'd been looking for.

That was part two of the plan.

44

I sprinted as fast as I could to Ye Olde
Fudge Factory, which was all the way on the other side of
Old Bridgetown, so I was totally out of breath when I got
there. Since it was still early, Bart the Fudgemaker was the
only one around. He was cooking something that smelled
so good it made my mouth *and* my eyes water.

"What are you making?"

Bart looked up from his huge pot. "Well, hey," he said.
Then he looked past me. "Where's the rest of your troop?"

"We're on our own today."

He eyed me suspiciously. "Really? They don't usually
allow that."

"Well, we're from a camp for gifted kids, so I guess that
makes us more responsible."

Bart thought that one over for a minute, then shrugged
and went back to his cooking.

"What are you making?" I repeated.

"Coconut fudge," Bart said, stirring what looked like
brown mud. "House specialty."

"Can I taste it?"

"It's not done."

"Please?"

Bart looked around, then took a small wooden spoon and dipped it into the melting chocolate. He handed it to me. "Blow on it first."

I blew for about half a second, then took a bite (more like a sip, actually). It burned my mouth a little, but I didn't care. It was quite possibly the single greatest thing I'd ever tasted. It was even better than the first time I discovered the combination of caramel and apple.

"Wow," I said. And then, for good measure, I added, "Wow, wow, wow, wow, wow."

"Yeah, it rocks the house," Bart said, still stirring.

I was begging Bart for another bite-sip when the door swung open. Dwayne and Lauren stood there.

"I knew it, the fudge factory!" she said, nodding excitedly.

Dwayne marched in and grabbed me by the collar, practically lifting me off the floor.

"*Is this your idea of a joke?*" he yelled. Without letting go of me, he got out his cell phone and pressed a button. "Yeah, I got him. Fudge factory." He hung up, glared at me again, then set his sights on Bart. "And what do you think you're doing, letting some kid wander in here by himself?"

Bart was too scared to speak, so I did. "Bart was just about to call the security people, he was just making sure he didn't start a fire first. He yelled at me, too."

Dwayne stared at Bart, but decided that he only had enough energy to be furious at one person. That would be me.

"All summer long we've put up with your shenanigans, because you seem like a good kid. And you actually did a brave thing with the Extra Workshop protest—that was pretty cool. But this is totally uncool. Totally uncool!" He looked at Lauren, who was still in the doorway. "You're lucky she told us where you were, or else we might have never found you, and you would have had to walk home."

"You would have found me, this place isn't that big," I said.

"That's not the point!" Dwayne was yelling now. *"You need to respect the rules!"* Dwayne shook his head. "I don't even want to know what kind of trouble you're going to be in."

Then, as if to answer Dwayne's question, Dr. Mal walked in. Ms. Domerca was right behind him.

Dr. Mal paced around the Fudge Factory for about a minute, not saying a word. Finally, I decided to start the conversation.

"I skipped the test because I don't belong here," I told

Dr. Mal. "Remember the first day, at the Welcome Ring, you said I was more like everyone here than I realized? Well, that was crazy then, and it's crazy now. It's the most obvious thing in the world. Kids come here because they love to read. I love to not read. So why don't we just call my coming to this camp a big mistake. In three hours my parents will pick me up and you'll never have to see me again."

Ms. Domerca stared at me with tears in her eyes. "I can't even begin to describe how disappointed I am in you," she said.

I so wanted to tell her everything. About Katie, about Zoe, about Lauren and Jared and our plan.

But I didn't.

"Obviously you will never be returning to our camp," Dr. Mal said. Then he looked at Lauren. "Thank you for your help. You're welcome to join the others for Final Workshop, if you'd like."

"I think I'll skip it," Lauren said, almost whispering. "I'm a little upset."

I looked at her. Man, she was good. Who knew?

Dr. Mal nodded. "Fine. Dwayne, please take them to the bus to wait for the others. Don't let Charlie Joe out of your sight."

"Will do, Dr. Malstrom," Dwayne said.

As we walked to the bus, Lauren took a quick glance at me.

Thank you, she said, without actually making a sound.

45

Dwayne, Lauren, and I waited on the bus alone for an hour and a half. No one said a word.

Eventually, the rest of the kids came out of the schoolhouse and got on the bus. They all completely ignored me. Katie wouldn't even look at me.

It was like I was right back where I started, on the first day of camp: a total outsider.

The only one who spoke to me was George.

"What happened?" he whispered. "Where were you? Is it true that you just decided to skip workshop and go to Ye Olde Fudge Factory? Are you kidding me? Who does that?"

I didn't answer any of his questions.

"We believed in you," George said. "We thought you were one of us."

When Jared got on the bus, he stared at Lauren for a second. Then

202

he went all the way to the back and sat by himself, staring out the window.

No one sang any arias—or any other kind of songs—the whole way back to camp.

Dear Mom and Dad,

By the time you read this, I will be back home, and probably grounded. I'm sure you won't believe me, but I actually got in trouble because I was helping a friend. I can't say any more than that.

Right now, I'm sitting in my cabin, and everything's packed up. In fifteen minutes we're going up to the flagpole to wait for the parents, and camp will finally be over. But guess what? I actually had a decent time at camp, and I made some good friends. And believe it or not, I was starting to think I might even want to come back here next year. Unfortunately, though, that's not possible now.

But that's okay, because helping a friend is way more important.

Your loving son,

Charlie Joe

46

Four hours later, everyone was standing in a giant circle around the flagpole, just like the first day of camp. But this time, it was called the "Farewell Ring." All the campers were there, of course. Except for one.

I was in Dr. Mal's office, looking out the window, waiting for my parents to pick me up.

I watched as the kids held hands and sang "Learning to Love, and Loving to Learn" for the last time. I watched as Dr. Mal went around and shook each camper's hand. I watched as all the parents started to pull up, get out of their cars, and hug their children. Nareem's parents. Katie's parents. George's parents. Cathy's parents. Jack's parents (and grandmother, complete with chocolate chip cookies wrapped in their usual five layers of tinfoil).

Then I saw my parents' car coming down the long dirt road. My mom was driving, my dad was in the passenger seat, and my sister Megan was in the back. Moose and Coco, our dogs, were fighting to stick their heads out the same window. You could tell by the excited looks on their faces that they knew they were coming to pick me up.

My dad got out of the car first. I saw him look for me, then scratch his head when he couldn't find me. I didn't want to watch anymore, so I sat down on the couch, staring at those six thousand diplomas again. A minute later Dr. Mal came in.

"Your parents are here. Let's go."

We headed outside. As soon as they saw me, my parents and sister ran up and hugged me.

"We missed you so much!" they all said, in some form or another. The dogs were barking like crazy, so I ran up to them and kissed and hugged them for about three minutes.

"Why were you waiting inside?" asked Megan.

Before I could say anything, Dr. Mal came up to my parents and reintroduced himself. Then he said, "We are just about to do the final announcements for the year, but afterward I would like to talk with you both for just a moment."

My parents looked at each other.

"Is there a problem?" my dad asked Dr. Mal. It seemed like with me, they always kind of expected the worst. For good reason, I suppose.

Dr. Mal flashed his friendliest smile. "Let's talk afterward, shall we?" Then he blew a whistle. "Announcements, please! Announcements!" he yelled, and everyone assembled around the flagpole, this time with parents in the mix.

"We've had a memorable summer here at Camp Rituhbukkee," Dr. Mal said. "A very interesting and unusual summer at times, certainly, but overall it was wonderfully rewarding. Thank you for entrusting us with your remarkable children."

People clapped and hugged, but the energy was low. Everyone seemed kind of wiped out from the morning's drama.

Dr. Mal went on. "And now, I'd like to announce the winner of our very first Rituhbukkee Reward." A hush fell over the circle. "As I mentioned on the first day of camp, this high honor goes to the camper who best displays the camp's core values of integrity, community, and scholarship. At stake is a full scholarship to next year's session." Dr. Mal paused. "The winner of the inaugural Rituhbukkee Reward is one of our finest campers, a person of compassion, kindness, and—as she showed just this morning—great responsibility. Please join me in congratulating Lauren Rubin."

People broke out in huge cheers. Everyone loved Lauren. She looked shocked. Her mom and dad were hugging, and her mom was crying. They looked so proud.

Lauren went up to Dr. Mal and shook his hand. Then Dr. Singer gave her a framed certificate. She looked at everyone, smiled, and headed back to her parents.

Then suddenly she stopped and walked back to Dr. Mal.

"I'm pretty sure I don't deserve this award," she told him. "Thank you for this incredible honor, but I can't accept it."

She handed him the certificate and then ran back to her parents and burst into tears.

Everyone froze in shock. After a second, Dr. Mal went up to Lauren and put his hand on her shoulder.

"Can you tell us what this is about?" he asked gently.

Lauren just shook her head. The whole camp was silent except for the sound of the wind in the trees. No one seemed to have any idea what to do next.

Except Jared Bumpers.

"It's his fault," he said, pointing at me.

Everyone stared at Jared, then turned to stare at me.

"You ruined everything," Jared continued, his eyes turning a little wild. "From the day you got here, to that stunt you pulled this morning, it's obvious you never belonged here. This whole summer's been messed up because of you."

"That's not true," I tried to say, but no words come out.

"You don't care about anybody but yourself," he said. "I figured that out when Dwayne was going to name me captain of the basketball team, but somehow you got him to change his mind and pick you."

"That's crazy!" I said, finding my voice. "I didn't even want to be captain!"

"And then, you made your big stand against Extra Workshop, just so you could be the center of attention," he went on. "You're lucky Katie figured out a compromise with Dr. Mal. You could have ruined everything for the rest of us!"

"I was—" I began, but didn't know how to finish the sentence. Everyone waited for Dr. Mal to say something, but I think he was too stunned to react.

Jared started walking around like he was a lawyer talking to a jury on one of those TV shows. "You came to this camp thinking you were way too cool for the rest of us," he said. "We're just a bunch of nerds at nerd camp, right? What's a popular kid like you doing here with the dorks, who like to read and write and actually want to make something of themselves?"

I looked at the people who had been my friends: Jack, George, Cathy. But none of them would look at me. Not after I skipped Final Workshop, which was an unforgiveable sin as far as they were concerned.

Jared smiled a cold smile. "You thought you could change us, get us to be more like you," he said. "Well, guess what? We know your type. Your type isn't welcome here. You proved it once and for all this morning by skipping the test. So you should just leave camp now before—"

"That's enough!" Lauren shouted. "Stop!"

Jared stopped.

Everyone turned to look at Lauren.

She stepped forward.

"Jared has no idea what he's talking about," Lauren began quietly. "Charlie Joe has more integrity in his little finger than Jared has in his whole body."

Jared's face turned white. It was as if he suddenly knew exactly what Lauren was about to say.

Her voice got stronger. "This morning, Charlie Joe did something that he knew would get him in huge trouble, but he did it anyway." Everyone looked at me. I stared straight ahead.

"But the amazing thing isn't that he did it," she continued. "Because we all know that's not exactly shocking behavior from this kid."

She took a deep breath.

"It's that he did it for me."

A gasp went through the crowd. I glanced at Katie, who had a look of total relief on her face.

"Charlie Joe Jackson skipped Final Workshop," she went on, "so I wouldn't have to cheat."

"Cheat how?" Dr. Mal asked.

Lauren stared at the ground. "Someone wanted to copy off my paper, and I didn't want to let them," she said, in a barely audible whisper. "But I probably would have, if Charlie Joe hadn't talked me out of it. His plan was just a way to help me."

Everyone stood there for a second. No one was quite sure what to do.

"Is this true?" Dr. Mal asked Lauren. "These are very, very serious allegations."

Lauren looked Dr. Mal right in the eye. "It's true," she answered.

Dr. Mal looked around the circle, until his eyes landed on Jared, who was starting to sweat through his shirt. Dr. Mal walked over and stood over him, the way he'd stood over me at The Welcome Ring on the very first day of camp.

"Mr. Bumpers," he said quietly, "do you have anything you'd like to tell us?"

Jared stared up at Dr. Mal for about ten seconds. He looked as if he were about to cry.

"I hate this freakin' place!" he finally shouted. Then he ran out of the circle and into the dining hall.

Nobody moved for about a minute. Then all at once, people started coming over and pounding me on the back happily. Katie practically jumped into my arms.

"I knew it," she kept repeating. "I just knew it."

The next voice I heard was my dad's.

"Are all nerd camps this weird?" he asked.

After about two minutes of buzzing, Dr. Mal cleared his throat and asked for everyone's attention.

"Okay, so now you know what I mean when I say this has been quite a summer," Dr. Mal said, as people laughed nervously. "But, even in these last five minutes, we've seen yet again what incredible kids we have at this camp. One camper is incredibly concerned because she is asked to cheat on behalf of a friend, and another camper sacrifices his good standing at the camp to help her. If that doesn't say a lot about the kind of kids we have, I don't know what does."

People started applauding. Quietly at first, then louder and louder, until it sounded like a huge wave. People kept clapping, while Lauren and I just stood there embarrassed. Finally Dr. Mal asked for quiet.

"That is why, after discussing it briefly with Dr. Singer, Dwayne, and Ms. Domerca, we have decided to offer not one, but *two* inaugural Rituhbukkee Rewards. Please join me in congratulating Lauren Rubin . . . and Charlie Joe Jackson."

I wasn't sure I heard him correctly. Did I just win a free

scholarship to attend Camp Rituhbukkee *again* next summer?!?

Gulp.

I suddenly got completely confused. Was this awesome or horrible? I had no idea.

Dr. Mal asked me if I wanted to say anything.

I did.

"Part of what Jared said is actually true," I said. "I hate to admit it, but when I first got here, I did think I was too cool for this place. In fact, I told myself that I needed to make you guys more like me. But that was just totally stupid. You guys are completely cool, in your own scary, dorky, nerdy, different kind of way." I looked directly at George and Jack. "And thanks for making me feel like I belong, even though you know that I totally don't."

Then I winked at Katie. She winked back.

I handed the microphone back to Dr. Mal. My parents hugged me. Megan hugged me. My dogs hugged me. And my friends who had been mad at me came up and hugged me, too.

"Well done," said Nareem.

"I knew you wouldn't just skip the test," said George. "I just knew it."

"This is totally going to help you get into college," said Jack. Before I could roll my eyes, he added, "Just kidding."

Ms. Domerca came up to me and gave me the biggest hug of all.

"You are quite the character," she said.

"Is that a good thing or a bad thing?" I asked her.

She laughed. "Both."

Dr. Mal came over and shook my hand.

"Congratulations, Mr. Jackson," he said. "We look forward to welcoming you back here next summer."

I looked him in the eye. I nodded. I smiled.

"Can't wait," I said.

I had no idea if I meant it or not.

A few minutes later, it was time to say good-bye. I started with Jack, who introduced me to his grand-mother, whom he called Nana.

"Jack's told me a lot about you," she said. "Most of it good."

"You make the best chocolate chip cookies ever created, Nana," I replied.

She winked at me. "You should try my plum cake." I didn't have the heart to tell her I hated plums.

Jack's parents were there, too. The famous Mr. Strong, who was really short but just as scary-looking as I'd imag-ined.

I shook his hand. "I've heard a lot about you, sir."

"Not all of it bad, I hope."

"Not all," I said. "Just most."

He let out a huge laugh for a split second. Then his eyes narrowed and he looked a little bit like he wanted to eat me.

I tried to ignore him and went up to Jack. "I have a going-away present for you," I told him.

He looked at me a little nervously. "You do?"

"Yup." I opened my duffel bag and pulled out one of my

favorite T-shirts. It had a picture of Homer Simpson on it, sitting on his couch with his belly out and chips and drinks spilled all around him. Above his head, it said AMERICAN IDLE.

"I want you to have this," I said, giving Jack the shirt.

He smiled nervously. "Thanks." He glanced down at the shirt he had on, which had a picture of a brain doing jumping jacks on it and the words TRAIN YOUR BRAIN.

Then he looked at his dad, who was checking out the Homer shirt with a suspicious look on his face.

Jack wasn't sure what to do next. He looked back at me.

"Think of Lech Walesa," I said.

Jack nodded, closed his eyes, and quickly took off his shirt.

"Jack, what are you doing?" asked his dad. But Jack didn't answer. Instead, he took a deep breath and pulled on the Homer Simpson shirt.

"Looks awesome," I said.

"Thanks," Jack said.

And we high-fived.

I still had a few farewells left.

First was Dwayne, who came up from behind me and gave me a bear hug, nearly breaking every bone in my body.

"The Jockstrap boys still don't know what hit them," he said, smiling. "Same time next year."

Lauren Rubin had a present for me: two pounds of Oreo cookie fudge from Ye Olde Fudge Factory.

I couldn't believe it. "When did you buy that?!?"

"When you weren't looking."

"Not possible," I told her. "There wasn't a single moment when I wasn't looking at that fudge."

Then I thanked her for about twenty minutes.

George was hanging on to Cathy Ruddy for dear life, so I decided to leave him alone. I'd text him later that night, now that my cell phone was back in its proper place—my pocket.

When I said good-bye to Ms. Domerca, I had to make sure I didn't cry.

"Charlie Joe said you were his favorite," my dad told her.

"He's one of my favorites, too," she said.

I held up the Lech Walesa book, which Ms. Domerca

said I could keep. "Ms. Domerca turned me on to this really good book about this really brave and interesting guy."

My parents stared at me. Ms. Domerca smiled.

"Kids can really surprise you, can't they?" she said.

"You can say that again," my mom answered.

"We taught Charlie Joe just a little bit about the joys of learning," Ms. Domerca said. "And he returned the favor by teaching all of us a little bit about the joys of *not* learning."

Katie and Nareem came over with their parents. They were holding hands.

"We made it," Katie said to me.

"Barely," I answered, and we laughed.

"See you at the beach?"

"Definitely."

"And at the library?" Nareem asked.

"Definitely not," I answered.

Katie's mom hugged me. "Will you really come back next year?" she asked.

"I have no idea," I answered.

Katie grinned. "Oh, he'll be here. This whole Lauren Rubin thing was just the final stroke of genius. That's how these secret nerds operate. He was dying to come back, and now he gets to come for free! Trust me, he planned the whole thing."

Everyone laughed.

Even me.

As we pulled away from camp, I looked around one last time. I took it all in: the basketball court, where we beat Camp Jockstrap; the Table Of Contents, where I worked on my newspaper articles; the dining hall, where I took a stand against Extra Workshop; and the lake, where Katie talked Dr. Mal into a compromise.

Then I looked at the flagpole, where camp began strangely, ended even more strangely, and I finally—kind of—became a true Rituhbukkean.

I sat in the back seat next to Moose and Coco, who both licked me as if I were a chocolate ice cream cone. Then I got out my cell phone and immediately texted Timmy, Jake, Hannah, Eliza, and Pete. The rest of the summer was going to be awesome!

So why was I feeling a little sad?

I put my phone away, took a deep breath, and closed my eyes, trying to deal with this weird sad feeling. When I opened them again, I saw the sign.

CAMP RITUHBUKKEE:

MOLDING YOUNG MINDS SINCE 1933

I stared at it, wondering if it was true. Had my mind been molded after all? It seemed like just yesterday I thought I'd landed on a distant, scary planet. Now, here I was, three weeks later, already kind of missing it.

Then I had an even scarier thought: Was Katie right? Was I really a nerd-in-training? Was the Lech Walesa book just the beginning?

Did I really like reading?

I let myself think about it for about five more seconds. Then I decided I'd done enough thinking for one summer.

So I ate a piece of fudge, lay my head down on Moose's lap, and slept the whole way home.

Dear Charlie Joe,

Since I didn't go to Final Workshop,
Ms. Domerca told me that my last assignment
was to write a letter to myself, to talk about
what I learned at camp.
    I learned that I definitely don't want to
write any more letters for a while.

Your pal,

Charlie Joe

"Learning to Love, and Loving to Learn"

The Camp Rituhbukkee Fight Song

We gather together on the lake's mighty shores
To make brand-new friendships, and open new
    doors
The summer is here now and yes, so are we
Let camp fill our hearts for all eternity.

Learning to love, and loving to learn
Time now to soar, like the earth's tallest fern
It's what makes the sun rise, what makes the
    world turn
Learning to love, and loving to learn.

Every book that we read gives us wisdom to
    spare
Every word that we write is a gift that we share
From the mountains to the valleys, let them all
    hear us sing
Knowledge is power, and power is king!
Learning to love, and loving to learn

Learning to love, and loving to learn
Time now to soar, like the earth's tallest fern
It's what makes the sun rise, what makes the
    world turn
Learning to love, and loving to learn.

* * *

"Wocka! Wockajocka!"

The Camp Wockajocka Fight Song

Wocka!
Wockajocka!
Wocka!
Wockajocka!
Wocka!
Wockajocka!
Wocka!
Wockajocka!
Wocka!
Wockajocka!
Gooooooooooooooooo Wockajocka!

ACKNOWLEDGMENTS

Free s'mores go to the following:

Nancy Mercado and Michele Rubin, for putting up with me and my half-empty glass.

Everyone at Roaring Brook/Macmillan, the best in the biz.

David Kane, trailermaster.

And Cathy Utz, for everything else.